MW01076695

ECSTASY

ALSO BY IVY POCHODA

NOVELS

Sing Her Down
These Women
Wonder Valley
Visitation Street
The Art of Disappearing

SHORT STORY

"Jackrabbit Skin"

ECSTASY

A NOVEL

IVY POCHODA

G. P. PUTNAM'S SONS
NEW YORK

PUTNAM
— EST. 1838 —

G. P. PUTNAM'S SONS
Publishers Since 1838
1745 Broadway, New York, NY 10019
An imprint of Penguin Random House LLC
penguinrandomhouse.com

Interior art: Dark seamless pattern © Alenarbuz / shutterstock.com

Library of Congress Cataloging-in-Publication Data

Names: Pochoda, Ivy, author.
Title: Ecstasy : a novel / Ivy Pochoda.
Description: New York : G.P. Putnam's Sons, 2025.
Identifiers: LCCN 2024040354 (print) | LCCN 2024040355 (ebook) |
ISBN 9780593851173 (hardcover) | ISBN 9780593851180 (epub)
Subjects: LCGFT: Horror fiction. | Novels.
Classification: LCC PS3616.O285 E37 2025 (print) |
LCC PS3616.O285 (ebook) | DDC 813/.6—dc23/eng/20241029
LC record available at https://lccn.loc.gov/2024040354
LC ebook record available at https://lccn.loc.gov/2024040355

Printed in the United States of America
1   3   5   7   9   10   8   6   4   2

Book design by Laura K. Corless

The authorized representative in the EU for product safety and compliance is
Penguin Random House Ireland, Morrison Chambers, 32 Nassau Street,
Dublin D02 YH68, Ireland, https://eu-contact.penguin.ie.

For Zoë Allen-Pohle,

who knows this story in the original

Off with your head
Dance 'til you're dead
Heads will roll
Heads will roll
Heads will roll
On the floor

—Yeah Yeah Yeahs,
"Heads Will Roll"

He is
pleased

if he can cause you to perform,
despite your plan,
despite your politics,

despite your neuroses,
despite even your Dionysian theories of self,
something quite previous,

the desire
before the desire,
the lick of beginning to know you don't know.

If life is a stage,
that is the show.
Exit Dionysos.

—Anne Carson,
"I wish I were two dogs
then I could play with me
(translator's note on euripides' *bakkhai*)"

ECSTASY

BEFORE

The young ones call me Mama Ghost because I've been at this so long.

I am a specter. A vampire. A night-creature.

You think I don't eat. You imagine I don't sleep.

I can see in the dark. I can hear what goes unsaid. I can hear your heart beat harder, faster than the DJ's dubstep, speed garage, trance buildups, jungle beats.

I've been there from the beginning—when the music was underground, when it was heavy, dark, and full of tribal calling. I was there for the first mainstream sounds, the candy and the kandi kids, the Technicolor dancers trading sticky necklaces and bug-eyed kisses on the dance floor. I'm there now, on the festival circuit, the commercial parties, the destination events. The three days of high-priced escape and brand-name DJs.

I'm there at bars. At after hours. At after–after hours.

I'm there when you need me. I keep your secrets. I've seen you at your worst. I know your bad habits. I've seen you beg and grovel. I've seen you plead for more, for favors, for just a taste.

I am your conscience. I am the devil on your shoulder. I am what you want, not what you need.

I've heard your desperate voice at 4 a.m. I've heard it at 7 a.m. I've heard it at noon. I can hear it even when you are stone-cold sober. I hear it when you are silent.

I hold the reins. I know exactly how much power I have to make your night or to ruin it. All of that in the palm of my hand—in the handoff, the hand-game—a quick palm to palm.

You put your life in my hands. Night after night. Party after party. I can make you invincible and I can kill you.

I can make you stay up all night and find god on the dance floor or in the mirror or in the bathroom stall or in the toilet or in the face of a stranger.

I've seen you weave tapestries from the air.

I've seen your fingers communicate in Morse code.

I can make you see. And I can blind you.

I can make you divine. I can destroy you.

But I look after you. I protect you. I keep you coming back.

I am your best friend and I always pick up when you call.

The young ones come and go. They attach themselves to me. They want to do what I do. They want my superhuman strength. They think that all it takes is the ability to stay up all night and sleep all day. They think that comes from handfuls of pills. Envelopes of powder. But it takes more than drugs to sell drugs. Especially when you're me—a woman.

You didn't expect that, did you? The first time you called? The first time someone pointed me out to you across the club, on the beach, at the back of the bar?

A woman. A mother. A wife.

Have you noticed that I'm sober when you're not? Have you noticed that I keep an eye on everything—that I'm keeping tabs, keeping track, keeping count, and keeping score. That I know who took what, who needs more, who has had too much?

You ever walked into the back room of the back room of the back room of a party at 3 a.m. to find seven guys on the wrong end of the night? Angry and amped, their attention—their fury and impatience—trained on you?

You ever been held up at gunpoint in an empty warehouse by a new supplier who wanted your cash?

You ever been pawed, patted, probed—fingers inside you—to make sure you weren't carrying a gun yourself?

You ever had to stand up to men twice your size, ten times as high, and forty times as brutal?

You probably think it's all parties and perks and VIP areas and backstage passes and comps.

You ever been raided? Surveilled?

Chased? Beaten? Choked? Cheated out of thousands of thousands?

You ever been caught at the UK border carrying five thousand pills destined for Creamfields and been offered a deal—flip on your suppliers and walk?

You ever sit there as they ask and ask and ask you to name names? As they isolate you and dehumanize you?

Three years I spent locked up in a foreign country at the mercy of guards and the sort of women I manipulated on the outside—the sort of women who begged and begged for a favor, a freebie, just one more. And then it was my turn for begging.

And that wasn't the worst of it.

My son. He turned me in.

I remember him at my arrest, wondering why he wasn't being taken in too.

The blood of my blood and all I am is his get-out-of-jail-free card.

You ever realize the only family you have left are the people you find in your never-ending after hours?

And you think you can do what I do?

What you don't know is that I left your world by choice. Once I learned to see around the edges of things, see behind and through things—see the self you keep hidden—I knew I would never go back. Once I could read the contrails on the dance floor. Once I was initiated into the dark heart of the dance. Once I learned it was possible to see more, see wildly, see without barriers and boundaries, why would I blind myself again, turn my back on spiritual rapture and pretend it was nothing more than a sport and a pastime?

If you believe god is a DJ, then I am your high priestess—the one who brings you close.

I will show you that the night has no borders, no beginning or end. I will tunnel you into yourself and help you hear that what's pumping in your veins isn't blood, it's trance. It's four-on-the-floor. It's dubstep. Handbag house. Darkcore.

You will know that I am the puppeteer of your secret self.

———

am the music and the party. I tune you in. I raise the goose bumps on your neck. I am the music's synesthesia—the glow-pulse that envelops you, tap-tap-tapping on your heart and skin.

I will save you and set you free.

I am everywhere and nowhere. And you will always think of me.

LENA

The domestic terminal at the Athens airport is dark and crowded. The seats hard. The smell of cigarette smoke barely contained in the plexiglass lounge across the room.

Lena shifts her weight. Her body aches from the San Francisco flight.

The puddle jumper to Naxos is late. There will be a delay— deplaning, cleaning the cabin, boarding. The usual.

She watches the first passengers come down the gangway—a gaggle of women. British? American? They are boisterous and loud. They wear flowing dresses and crowns—the cheap tourist kind, the metal laurel wreaths sold at every shop in Greece. Some have flowers tangled in their hair.

The women link arms, singing, as they approach the passengers waiting to board.

They pass in front of Lena. She catches the stink of vacation— sunscreen and the deep funk of wine.

One of them—wild haired, her dress askew, her crinkled, freck- led breasts barely contained in her sundress—trails a finger across Lena's cheek as she passes. The woman's finger lingers on Lena's chin. Her scent is strong—earthy, mossy, a feral crawl through a cave. Mud and sweat and something Lena can't quite place. The salt lick of the sea. She can hear something too—drumbeats and the ocean. A chant and a dance. A taste in her mouth—blood or wine, deep and rich, delightful and deadly.

For the first time in years, she feels the desire to dance. She feels the loosening of her limbs. The syncopation of her arms and legs.

She opens her mouth, as if to drink the woman's air.

Then the scent fades.

Lena rises to her feet, her hand outstretched to pull the woman back. Her mouth still open.

Then a restraining hand on her arm. She hits the chair, her purse tumbling to the ground.

"Jesus, Mom. Close your mouth. What the hell." Her son, Drew—his dead father returned to life. "Is there a lounge around here somewhere or does this shithole terminal not even have that?"

The smell, the sound, the taste—vanished. Still, something remains—a note, a last beat of Lena's heart before it's all gone.

"The look on your face, Mom. You look deranged."

Lena cranes her neck hoping for one more glimpse. She rises again. Her head swiveling—a frantic pinwheel. Her hands, once so graceful. Her body—they had called it musical.

"Stop, now." Drew's hand on her again. "They should have a separate terminal for drunk vacationers. Separate airlines."

"They do." Drew's wife, Jordan. Picture-perfect in a white linen dress, straight black hair, gold sandals. Not pretty though. Too cold for true beauty. "They fly low cost. À la carte drinks and no frills. It's a good business model. But with some flaws. For instance . . ."

Drew's hand leaves Lena and reaches for his wife. "Every business model has shortcomings."

"Yes, but," Jordan says. Yale undergrad and JD/MBA from Harvard. Her father the CFO of British Airlines, her mother a former flight attendant. "The low-cost model is beset by both employee strikes and unresolved passenger complaints, not to mention scaling baggage policies, which has led to—"

"The real problem," Drew says, "is allowing them to share terminal space. It's like waiting for a limo and having to watch a Greyhound bus arrive. Dad would be horrified."

But "Dad" is dead. Found on the beach dune below the hotel he was developing. *Like he'd been struck down*, the worker who discovered him had reported.

The island coroner ruled his death a heart attack.

The airport is noise and congestion. Anxious summer travelers. Hungry children. Irritated adults. Everyone in the here and now—checking the time, checking the monitors, worried about delays and connections—nothing like the women who just passed through.

"I don't mind the terminal," Lena says. Too many years of being cloistered and sequestered. The loneliness of luxury. Private dining rooms. Blacked-out windows of town cars. Cab-to-curb service.

"You grew up flying coach, so that tracks," Drew says.

"Drew." Jordan bristles. "Don't be such a snob."

"Pointing out facts is not snobbery. It's facing reality. My mother grew up flying coach."

"I enjoyed it," Lena says. "It was an adventure. Something you'll never understand."

Despite flying first class from San Francisco last night, her back is sore. Her calves are tight.

"At least on the island, we'll be kept away from women like

those," Drew says, removing his hand from Jordan and waving toward the airport exit. "Whatever they got up to on their *vacation*, they're too old for it."

Vacation—as if it's a dirty thing done by dirty people.

Jordan and Drew don't vacation—they travel.

"Too old for what?" Hedy has returned from the smokers' lounge, her eyes hidden behind large designer sunglasses—saucer-sized tortoiseshell frames that forbid entry.

"Too old to be so drunk in public."

"No one is too old for anything," Hedy says, patting Drew's head before sliding off to talk to the gate attendant.

Drew smooths his hair. "Those sunglasses make her look hungover."

Jordan waves a hand in front of her face as if Hedy brought all the smoke from the lounge with her.

"She's going blind," Lena says. "Macular degeneration."

"I've heard," Drew says.

"She shouldn't smoke," Jordan says.

Lena watches Hedy chatting with the gate attendant, waving an arm stacked with cheap bangles. "No one *should* smoke."

Thirty-five years ago, Hedy burned so bright she was blinding. A party unto herself. A late night that turned and turned and never wore out. She and Lena had met in the company of the Frankfurt ballet. Lena was a workhorse—the best dancer in Ohio—but not as naturally talented as the others, always aware of her limitations. Hedy had no limits except those of her own making—the ones that led to weight gain and injury. That led to giving up shortly after Lena was let go.

So they traveled. They hitchhiked to Morocco. They accepted invitations to New Year's in Moscow. They put Ibiza to shame.

Back then Hedy hid behind cheap drugstore frames—disguising the aftermath of the nights that didn't end as she broke so many dawns she shattered calendars. A drama queen, of course. Louder, livelier than everyone else. The sunglasses were part of it all.

Then came the upgrade—sunglasses worn even while sober. Her eyes hurting. Always hurting. Tripping on the street. Crashing her car.

Rumors that she was out of control. No longer a party person but a drunk. No longer amusing but an addict.

By the time Hedy received her diagnosis at twenty-six, Lena had already stumbled into a hasty marriage. Chosen extreme financial stability over the wild nights, the hostels, the children-of-god-Goa-trance-full-moon mania.

Aren't you glad you stopped wasting your twenties, Stavros said to her on their wedding night. She should have known right then.

I didn't waste a day. But she didn't say it, certain that he knew better. He hadn't wasted his twenties. He'd dropped out of hospitality school in Hartford, Connecticut, and built an empire. Impressive for the son of an immigrant cabdriver. Not all of it was on the level—but those were secrets Lena learned to keep. *Business is dirty*, Stavros had told her. *But our lives are clean.*

She and Hedy drifted.

They saw each other every few years—more awkward each time. Lena dressed in smart tapered pants, Hermès bangles, luxe flats. A costume at first. Then armor against the realization she'd made a mistake. Hedy in harem pants, a knockoff bag trimmed with things that dangled and chimed, platform sneakers. But always designer sunglasses. *By the time I'm sixty—lights out*, she told Lena. *By then I'll have seen everything.*

A collectible—that's what Lena had become.

Nearly all of Stavros's friends had one—a dancer or a petite violist who hadn't made the cut. A tidy curiosity. There was Walter Salmon in Bermuda married to a Muscovite ballerina who defected for a better life in a Caribbean fortress. There was Leonard Stillman in Texas, who snagged the lead violist from the Shanghai Philharmonic. And Stavros, who got Lena and never revealed that she hadn't made the cut at the Frankfurt ballet.

Small mercies.

Drew stands, checking on whatever Hedy is up to at the gate. This is his show. His trip. Lena and Hedy are only along for the ride as he slides into his father's shoes, finishing what Stavros started.

He was always Stavros's child more than hers.

She stares at her son's profile. He's got her ruddy American complexion and a softness to his face. But he has his father's eyes—unyielding and inflexible. And the same determined set to his mouth.

She wonders what else Drew inherited from Stavros. A dexterity with loopholes, maybe. A ruthless way with others.

Time will tell, Lena figures. Drew has just stepped into the role of CEO of Stavros's international hotel chain. Never a thought of Lena getting involved. No real desire on her part either.

She'd thought that Stavros's untimely death on a Greek island would free her from her obligations to the company, but here she is.

Lena watches as Drew inserts himself between Hedy and the desk, an authoritarian body block.

Hedy retreats. "He thinks wealth can make the plane take off quicker," she says as she flops down next to Lena.

"It's been known to happen," Jordan says.

Jordan's tone, clipped and well informed. Clinical and dismissive. Not what Lena had expected in a daughter-in-law. What she wanted was an ally. What she got was an emotional bureaucrat.

Lena watches her son return to their bank of seats. She has to admit he has some of his father's elegance, though tempered by her flat American tone. Still, he impresses her.

He takes a seat on the far side of Jordan—a glance at her belly. Three months pregnant, but hard to tell beyond a small distortion of her waistline. Blessedly still able to join them on this trip, according to Drew, who follows the rules of prenatal care to a T. As if it's his body. As if his decisions can affect their child.

Hedy removes her glasses, polishes them quickly. Her eyes are milky. Their deep sapphire hue gone cloudy and vague. Cataracts on top of degeneration.

"Did you see them? Those women?" Lena asks.

"They sounded like they had some sort of island fever. Vacation overload. We were like that I bet."

"Jesus," Drew says. "Please."

"We were twenty," Lena says.

"Not all twenty-year-olds run wild," Drew says.

"We were amazing." Hedy replaces her glasses. "It's never too late."

"It is," Lena replies. A look at Drew. His protective hand around Jordan's shoulder, as if shielding her from Hedy and Lena.

LENA

They fly first class on the puddle jumper from Athens to Naxos. Their seats are the same as in economy, just wider spaced. A curtain separates them from the other vacationers.

Hedy and Lena sit across the aisle from Drew and Jordan. The flight attendant passes through with complimentary champagne. A stiff shake of Drew's head. Jordan holds up a palm and shrinks back into her seat, Drew's hand now clasping hers. A squeeze of approval.

Hedy leans across the aisle. "It won't kill you, you know."

"She's fine," Drew says.

"When I was pregnant I was a health nut, earth mother. I only ate organic, meditated every day, ran from the mere thought of cigarette smoke. Julia was stillborn. Lena on the other hand enjoyed herself, had a drink now and then. Or rather more often than not. And look—Drew's a CEO and double-barreled Ivy grad."

"Only now and then," Lena says. Just to numb the pain of her body betraying her, growing, slowing, expanding. "Sometimes. And only a single glass."

A snort from Hedy.

"I'm just saying," Hedy says. "No harm in loosening up. It's a vacation, right?"

A flicker of discomfort passes across Jordan's face. "Thank you," she says, pulling closer to the window.

"Don't thank me. What I'm telling you is that there's no rhyme or reason behind it all. You never know what you'll get but either way a glass of champagne isn't going to flip the script."

"It turned out that Mother didn't want children," Jordan says. "So I—"

"So she's determined to course-correct. Do everything right," Drew says.

"Shame about the bubbly," Hedy says, rising from her seat. "It settles the stomach." She disappears down the aisle. A quick stagger, then rights herself.

"Hedy's daughter was stillborn," Drew says, "because she had a failed abortion."

Lena scowls at him across the aisle. The things you tell your son when you imagine he will be your best friend.

She's raised an asshole. Not that he cares what she thinks.

"She was a dancer too? I didn't think dancers smoked," Jordan says.

"She hasn't been a dancer for years." Drew's voice cold and final.

"We all grow old," Lena says.

Except. Except there is still some of that spark in Hedy—despite her excess flesh and her chunky clothes that conceal her shape and weigh her down. Somehow, she still has the grace and the carriage. She's got the command and the flair.

Lena is too brittle these days. Too regimented from years of sitting politely at attention at dreary dinners. From perching on high heels at charity galas. Hard to imagine what her body once did. Hard to feel how the music once flowed inside her—inspiring the elegant ripple of her arms, the sweep of her legs, the leaps and twirls.

Carrying Drew had ended all that—stolen her grace, weighed her down. A pregnancy that had broken her three decades ago.

O ut the window the sea is picture-postcard lapis—slight waves catching golden curls of sunlight.

Lena and Hedy had gone to Greece together. Crete. Twenty-two and totally broke, their last cash spent on the cheap airfare and a package hotel deal. Their plan—to rely on the comfort of strangers to buy them drinks poolside at swanky resorts.

They didn't know this would be their last hurrah—that their plan would work so well that Lena would entrap Stavros, or was it the other way around, and she'd never have to worry about paying for a drink again.

The moments you can mark in time. The first four days on Crete. The last four days that Lena had been Lena and not some-body's fiancée, somebody's wife, somebody's mother. The last four days filled with unrestricted movement and untethered freedom.

Who are we without other people in our lives? We are ourselves. But we seek unions and duties and attachments that chip away at us until we are half a person—half someone else. Nobody to our-selves.

Things you realize too late. Or perhaps don't even realize at all. Maybe they just linger at the back of your mind, tapping away, al-ways present, despite the luxury hotels, the grand vacations, the country house, and the city town house and penthouse. More clothes than you need or want. More things to distract from the fact that you aren't enjoying the ones you have. Blessings are double-edged. Always a trade-off in the end. Always a price to pay.

There was a moment when she had loved Stavros. When he had dazzled her with everything that she'd thought she wanted— ushering her into a decadent world of culture and art and society that she'd never have reached as a company dancer. Making her feel refined without having to struggle in the studio until her feet were bleeding. He took that pain away. Made her life easy. Tricked her into thinking she was still important. Told her that dance was too much work, too unstable. That being a patron was more worthwhile than being a performer. He promised her she'd have more control, more sway and say.

And she believed him because she needed to. She had seen the vanishing point of her dancing days approaching. Stavros just accelerated its arrival.

But it was a trick. He took the pain of failure away and replaced it with another.

She had tried to continue loving him. But sometimes that meant hating herself.

Drew was a different story. You love your kids regardless. So much like his father, but still.

Hedy returns to her seat with a jolt.

The plane is making its descent, a large arc across the island before doubling back to the small airport. The sky is clear, the water, the harbor, the mountain towns perfectly visible. And then an air pocket. The plane plummets, maybe only a few feet but enough to raise a cry from the passengers.

Lena presses against the window, imagining she could find the beach where Stavros met his end. Imagining that it would be visible from ten thousand feet.

Up to her, they would have taken a ferry from Athens, giving them time to acclimate and appreciate. Feel the power of the sea—get some understanding of place and space, some respect for the majesty of the water.

Imagine asking Drew to sit on a ferry for six hours.

Imagine asking him to line up with the other *vacationers*.

Imagine asking him to be one of them.

Another plummet. This one jacking up Lena's heart rate. Summoning sweat from her palms.

It feels as if the plane is being sucked down, pulled toward the island.

And then calm, as if nothing at all. The plane levels, glides into its smooth descent.

Drew tries to be a gentleman like his father, but it always feels forced, like a pantomime rather than an imperative. He helps Jordan off the plane. Her face—pale, tight. He helps Hedy with her bags. Lena takes care of herself. Self-sufficient after fifty. Independent at last.

A car is waiting for them. An SUV, rare on the islands. The driver in uniform. Stavros would be pleased.

There's a quick gasp of fresh air—a blast of the salt-and-basil smell of the islands and the sun's drunk warmth. Then they are in the climate-controlled car. The windows darkened, reducing their first passage through Naxos to a polarized blur.

The Agape Villas was Stavros's last investment—costly and a little reckless. Nevertheless, a place, he told Lena, where he would cultivate tradition and memory. But she knew the real reason was to erase his pedestrian upbringing as a firstborn immigrant in a third-rate American city and rewrite his own history. Return to Greece as an entrepreneur, a person of weight and importance. Establish himself as a favorite son.

The hotel had been in development for three years. Stavros had promised it was going to be an easy build. The government had slashed red tape for international investors and bond rates had dropped to record lows. People were flocking to the lesser-known islands in search of sustainability and authenticity. He promised he would ride the wave of a booming Greek hospitality sector. But there were hurdles that kept him up all night. Problems from the ground up—issues with everything from plumbing to cultural preservation. Too much for Lena to digest or comprehend. The less she knew the better because knowledge about Stavros's business never soothed her.

But under Drew's short tenure, it's done at last—the project Stavros didn't see to completion. The one that killed him, Lena suspected. The Agape Villas—twelve whitewashed buildings on a hill overlooking one of Naxos's famed beaches. Behind them some of Greece's finest vineyards. Secluded. Luxurious. But in tune with the island. At least that's what Stavros said on their last call before his death.

The car rambles through several of the island's picturesque towns that Lena knows are filled with winding cobbled streets, boutiques selling hand-embroidered dresses, some peddling machine-made knockoffs.

Drew will avoid these places. Avoid the cafés and the crowded beaches with tourists taking selfies against the rosy-fingered sky. She will be cloistered. It will be as if Stavros is reaching from beyond the grave to improve on her wishes until they match up with his own.

Less than a year into her marriage, she'd begun to feel smothered. The suffocation of comfort. It fits tight, like a noose. With Stavros gone, Lena had hoped to breathe freely. But her son is now her puppeteer.

They approach the hotel.

"I want to smell the sea," Hedy says. "Can you roll down the window?"

The driver lowers the windows on the inland side. "Our vineyards are up to the right, above the hotel."

"The sea," Hedy says.

"We want our guests' first impression of Agape to be a view of the hotel, not the view from the hotel."

"Why can't I see the water?" Hedy asks.

"Just look at the hotel, Hedy," Drew says.

Hedy leans over her seat toward Drew. "Why?"

"Dammit," Drew says.

Lena reaches out to her son—to what? Restrain him? Calm him?

"Drew, Hedy wants to see the beach."

"The first view should be of the hotel," Drew says. His tone unusually harsh, even for him.

She gets it. The beach—where his father died.

"It's okay, Hedy," Lena says. "We can see the beach tomorrow."

"Maybe," Drew says. "There are a few final touches that aren't quite ready. So, for now, just take a look at the hillside."

"I thought everything was done," Jordan says.

"Nothing is ever done in this business," Drew says. "You should know that."

Lena knows too. After all, she's lived with this business for more than three decades. And she knows, from Drew's tone, that there's more to this story.

"I do," Jordan says. "I'm just going off what you said."

A deep breath from Drew. "It's just a few small things that need to be ironed out."

Another tone of Stavros's that Lena recognizes. He's holding something back, blurring or manipulating some facts.

"It will be fine," Drew says.

The car turns away from the unseen sea and begins the climb—a well-paved, twisting approach that mimics a donkey path. A switchback that alternates between the sea view and the mountain view—if only the windows were down.

It's a relief to step out of the car, to feel the elements.

There are twelve villas, for the nine muses and three graces, the driver explains, holding the SUV door open.

Hedy loops her arm through Lena's, lets Lena guide her.

Gracious white architecture that seems part of the landscape but also alien, otherworldly. Classical but modern. A large infinity pool hovers at the edge of the property, overflowing but never emptying.

"Each room has a private pool," Drew says. "You'll be more comfortable there."

"I don't mind the communal one," Lena says. "Might be fun."

"Mom, I want you to relax. I want you to experience the luxury Dad intended."

For years her body on display in leotards, onstage, in bikinis. And now hidden away.

Hedy lowers her glasses, rolls her milky eyes. Time rewinds more than three decades. The two of them hitching a ride—their driver unaware that the young women had no interest, that when they danced to the music at a rest stop, the dance was not for him. That he was a means to an end. A source of laughter. A joke that would be told all night and for the rest of the vacation. *The luxury Dad intended.*

The concierge and some of the staff are lined up outside the entrance. Lena breathes deeply, drinking the fresh air, her lungs cold and canned after nearly twenty-four hours of air-conditioning. She'd like to sit down right there, let the sun hit, the sky blind, let the distant waves break and echo. She wants to sit and stay and absorb it all before entering her cloister.

Lena realizes with a cold shiver that she already knows the drill. Everything will be looked after. Everything thought of on her behalf. Everything anticipated. Meals she doesn't have to order. Drinks she didn't know she wanted.

Inside this hotel her thoughts, her wishes, will not be her own.

Stavros is haunting her.

She had always imagined vacation as an escape from the everyday. But it was—and will be—as confining as the air in their Pacific Heights mansion and Upper East Side penthouse.

Being rich means never being alone.

It means being surrounded by whispering workers—the housekeeper and her staff. The nanny and the night nurse, the babysitter and the driver. The assistants and their assistants. The security cameras and nanny cameras and doorbell cameras and phone monitors. Someone always watching.

The Agape will be the same.

———

In the foyer there are trays of chilled Greek wine *from our vineyards*. A platter with canapés of olives and farmer cheese. There is a cobbler to craft bespoke Greek sandals. There is a perfume butler to capture the guests' preferred island scent. There is a catalogue of artwork they may rent for their suites.

Every detail considered and patiently explained. There will be nothing to worry about. Nothing to think about. No choices to make.

Lena and Hedy accept another glass of wine.

The escort party is ready to lead them to their rooms. Their bags will follow if they did not already proceed silent and unnoticed.

Hedy stumbles. "Light-headed," she says.

"Maybe cool it with the wine," Drew says.

Lena tightens her grip on Hedy. "You don't need to monitor us."

She watches Drew exchange a look with Jordan.

On their way through the lobby, the manager describes the careful decor—the craftsmanship, the sourcing, the modernized authenticity, the whitewash, the limestone, the inlay, the painted mosaic ceiling in the foyer—the muses and the graces—that took two thousand hours of work, describing it all in excruciating detail.

Boring.

Hedy doesn't even have to say it. Lena reaches for her hand.

"Mom, you're in Villa Terpsichore. It's the grandest. The highest up. Wraparound balcony. Your own infinity pool. I worked hard on the art program for the hotel. We collaborated with local painters. You'll see the results in your suite."

"If it's the grandest, it should be yours," Lena says.

He puts his hand on hers. "It's all arranged."

"But I don't need—I don't want . . ."

"How do you know what you don't want if you don't even know what it is?"

"Since when did you start making decisions for me?" Lena says.

"It's what Dad did."

"And who told you I liked it?"

"You never said you didn't."

There's truth to that. A lot. No one ever accused Drew of missing a beat.

They face off in the lobby.

"All I'm saying is that I don't need the grandest room." Terpsichore—the muse of dance. Perhaps the villa should be Hedy's.

"Everything was taken care of weeks ago," Drew says. "It's ridiculous to shuffle things now. If you had cared about the arrangements, you could have showed some interest before we left. Just enjoy the ride."

"I'd like to have some say in the ride," Lena says.

Drew takes her half-full wineglass and puts it on the tray.

"I'll have another," Hedy says, reaching for the tray.

"Make sure you can stay on your feet, Hedy," Drew says.

Hedy raises the glass. "Don't worry, darling. Wine alone can't take me down."

The villa is too much, as Lena knew it would be. She stands in the middle of the sitting room, waiting for her luggage. She kicks off her shoes to feel the cool tile. A flat-screen TV is cleverly concealed behind a painting of the muses.

There's a couch and a swing. A bar. A dining table for ten. Replica amphorae, each one showing a classical Greek chorus, holding dried stalks of lavender.

In each room—a button to summon service.

Three bedrooms, even though there is only one of her.

The white walls are trimmed in geometric patterns in gold-leaf paint.

Everything white and cool—the couches, the beds, the curtains. Paintings of ancient dancers on two walls.

Outside the arched windows is her private infinity pool with recliners in the shallow end. Lena mistakes the water sloshing from the pool for the sea, which is probably the point.

There's another dining area outside. A driftwood table, also for ten, and an outdoor kitchen.

A party palace.

Lena has never felt more alone.

Dinner is at Drew's—Villa Erota. Similar to Lena's but angled differently. A different sea view. A different configuration of rooms. A subtle love theme in the decor. Artwork of Eros and Aphrodite—all of it commissioned for the Agape.

They sit outdoors and eat early. The sun gone orange, dyeing the water a sherbet rainbow. The spread is lavish. The service immaculate.

The rhythmic falling of the infinity pool draws Lena away from the meal—lulls her. Too much wine. Too much travel. Everything with Stavros, and now Drew, always too much.

Those women at the airport—their boisterous joy. Carrying their vacation into the real world. Where had they stayed? Where had they come from?

Then her son's voice from miles off. "How do you like your room, Hedy?"

"You could fit an entire family in there. And maybe you should."

Drew's cold laugh. "And the pool? You've probably never had a private pool before."

Lena can hear the wine rolling in her son's voice.

"I wouldn't mind sharing the common one," Hedy says. "I'm easygoing."

"Oh no," Drew says. "This way you and my mom won't have to seduce rich men into buying you drinks."

So strange—his father's tease coming out of his mouth.

Then silence.

The lap-lap of the pool. The sound of Drew replacing his glass. A scrape of a chair. "That's what you did, isn't it? That's how you and Dad met. Right, Mom? You and Hedy were working a pool in Crete or somewhere. God, Jordan, did I even tell you this story?"

"You make it sound as if we were hookers," Hedy says.

"We were twenty-two. It wasn't an outrageous thing to do," Lena says. "In fact, I'd say it was fun."

How old is Jordan? Twenty-eight? Not far off from twenty-two.

"How did *your* parents meet, Jordan?" Hedy asks.

She damn well knows the answer. She and Lena had been laughing about it since the wedding. The CFO of British Airlines and the stewardess. *That's some* Pretty Woman *shit right there*, Hedy had said.

"They met at work," Drew says.

"My mother was tired of her day job and traded up," Jordan says.

"Traded up!" A snort from Hedy. "More like dug gold."

"Hedy!" Lena kicks her under the table.

Jordan looks at Lena over her water glass. "She saw a good deal and took it. You know how that goes."

Lena nearly chokes on her wine. "Excuse me?"

"It's what you did, isn't it? Do you think people should look down on you for your choices?" Jordan asks.

They don't need to, Lena thinks. She's got that covered all by herself.

Drew leans over the table, leering at Lena. "Mom, how many men did you go after at a time? Did you cast a wide net or did you home in on the rich ones?"

"Drew, we were young and having fun."

"You tricked him. Admit it. It was a trap."

"Maybe he trapped me."

"Don't be ridiculous," Drew says.

"Is it so hard to imagine your father falling in love with me when I was twenty-two?"

"She was so beautiful," Hedy says. "She still is. Lena, you still are."

Drew narrows his eyes at Lena over his wineglass. "You gave him what he wanted. He gave you what you wanted."

"Well, that is sort of the definition of love, sweetheart," Lena says.

"No, Mom. That is the definition of transactional."

"Getting dashing rich men to buy you drinks is hardly transactional," Hedy says. "It's a time-honored tradition for young women."

"Jordan was young once and she didn't do things like that." Drew's arm around her shoulder again.

"I learned from my mother's mistakes," Jordan says.

"Sounds like your mother had her eye on the ball," Hedy says. "Sounds like she knew a good time."

"She thought she did. But she was wrong," Jordan says.

Lena has heard this story in bits and pieces. A chilly upbringing in London. Off to boarding school before most kids had their first sleepovers. Then to America for the Ivory Tower.

Jordan puts a hand on the small swell of her belly. "Speaking of a good time, that's exactly what I'm hoping to do before—"

"Before your life ends," Hedy says.

A dark flash in Jordan's eyes.

Hedy slugs her wine. "Lighten up, Jordan, it's a joke."

"Her life won't end, Hedy," Drew says. "Only someone who doesn't understand the joys of parenting could say something like that."

"And you understand those joys?" Hedy's speech is dangerously slurred.

"He's right," Lena says. "She'll have all the help she needs. Night nurse. Day nurse. Postpartum doula. Drivers and laundry and anything and everything all at once."

"You say that as if it's a bad thing," Jordan says.

Drew refills his glass. "You had all those things, Mom. And did your life end? No, it didn't." A decisive thunk of the bottle back on the table—a gavel that decides it.

A look from Hedy. "Lena?"

Hedy knows, of course—the frustration, the isolation that drove Lena to sneak drinks and the occasional smoke regardless of conventional wisdom, to call Hedy at all hours because she knew Hedy would be awake. To dissolve into tears over her swelling belly or her sleepless infant while Hedy described the club she had been to, rabbiting on at a mile a minute, the drugs ramping her speech up to 100 rpm.

"My life didn't end, of course," Lena says. "It changed."

"And now it's changing back." Hedy reaches for her hand and clasps her fingers, raising them above her shoulders. "You're coming down to earth. And you are going to be the rich one buying your young foolish suitors drinks."

"No, she won't." Drew manhandles his wineglass, nearly crashing it into his teeth.

"Maybe I will," Lena says. "What else should I do?"

"Mom." Then out of the corner of his mouth, "Jesus, what's gotten into you? Dad's been gone for less than three months and already you're acting like a loose cannon."

"It's a joke, Drew."

A moment of silence.

"Anyway, we've got the hotel to ourselves so there's no danger of me buying a drink for anyone."

"And we have a state-of-the-art security system that can lock your rooms from the front desk should anyone try to intrude," Drew says.

And they are back on track, back in their places.

After dinner Drew walks Lena to her room. "Be careful, Mom." A kiss on the cheek.

A moment of actual concern from her son.

"Are you worried I'm going to die down on the beach too?"

"What? No. Dad was a huge presence. Life without him will be disorienting until you find your footing again."

Of course, how could she have been so silly. Drew's not worried about her—he's worried about her embarrassing him.

Lena closes the door, seals herself in her empty palace.

She imagines Drew on the other side, waiting, keeping vigil, making sure she doesn't escape.

Before bed Lena switches off the air-conditioning, opens the doors to the porch, pulls back the white linen curtains. Lets in the sea air and the night noise. Lets in the dark. The wild-basil scent and the distant drums. Or is it the ocean? Or is it—but Lena is too tired to think, too tired for anything save letting the night wash over her, carrying, carrying, and then sleep.

She dreams of the women in the airport.

She dreams of the woman who stroked her cheek. She can smell her—feral, floral, and wild. A little bit delicious.

She feels the pulse in each of the woman's fingertips. Feels the heartbeat-drum. The blood. Its pressure and rhythm.

The woman comes closer. Her lips near. Her breath—ragged. A word, a secret, something hovering. A confession.

Then she bites. Her mouth clamping on Lena's chin. The skin splitting as the woman shakes side to side—a fiercer, deep grip on her prey. Lena's blood—a fountain gushing, flowing, filling the stranger's mouth. Until she is drained and dreamless.

LENA

Breakfast arrives unbidden and is served poolside. It's a spread for a family, although Lena eats alone. A trio of cheeses. A tower of fruit. Assorted breads and honeys. A salad of cucumber and tomato. A small platter of desserts. A modest carafe of wine.

This is what it will be like from here on out—Lena alone in a world of too much, rambling around the Pacific Heights mansion and the Upper East Side penthouse, residences so big they require a staff.

Maybe she'll fire everyone when she gets home. Maybe she'll let her residences go. Run them to ruin.

Or maybe she'll sell them. The idea so revolutionary, so unhinged, it raises Lena's spirits so high she feels as if she could float toward the ceiling.

What is she always being urged to do by the motivational speakers at her ladies' luncheons—*let go of things that do not serve me, hold on to things that spark joy.*

———————

There's a massive bouquet of flowers and a note from Drew. *The boat to dinner leaves at five.*

Lena slips on one of the robes hanging in the closet. Time to wash off the travel—the airports and transfers and smell of everyone else. She puts her hand to her chin. There is no bite. Not even a bruise, no remnant of some oneiric accident where dream and reality collided.

Before she can get in the shower, there is a massage—also unbidden, unexpected, and poolside. If she doesn't object, tomorrow there will be a Reiki healing. The next day a guided meditation. The next, chakra balancing.

After twelve days, Lena will be relaxed into submission.

Hedy is outside the door—a massage-oil sheen on her arms and neck. She's wearing dark amber-tinted glasses the size of hockey pucks. "Let me in or I'll die of boredom. I swear."

"Keep your voice down," Lena says.

"Or what, you'll call the management? You are the management. You are the owner. Top of the food chain. Get the other guests kicked out if you want."

"There aren't any other guests. Not until we are officially open."

"Even better," Hedy bellows. "Even less reason to keep it down."

Lena ushers her outside. Why the urge to be polite? Why the urge to play by abstract rules?

"What's wrong?" Hedy says, removing her cover-up and revealing a monokini in clashing animal prints. "You look like a housewife who accidentally polished off the last of her husband's booze. You used to be—fun. Especially on vacation."

The size and shape and color of Hedy. The abundance. The mess and disorder. The too-much and the too-loud and the just-right. Her feet, still dance damaged after all these years. Her calves still muscled.

"I'm going to sell the houses."

"Good for you," Hedy says.

Lena's eyes trail down her friend's body. "Can you still get on pointe?"

"Stop staring at me and get in the goddamn pool. And get one of your minions to send up some wine. Adult size this time. Not that baby bottle they sent with breakfast."

The wine hits hard.

The sun.

The massage.

The travel and the jet lag.

Hedy and Lena circle each other in the pool.

"I was fun," Lena says. "What happened?"

"It didn't have to happen."

"Women our age aren't allowed to be fun."

"Speak for yourself," Hedy says.

Lena hauls out poolside, lies on the limestone. Everything is ridiculous—the infinity pool, the concierge service, her bespoke luggage, her caftans, her designer everything. "I'm bored. I'm so fucking bored."

"Let's go to the beach."

"Oh my god, yes," Lena says. "What the fuck are we doing in this shithole?"

---

biza. Tulum. Bali. Goa. Costa Rica. Barcelonita. Sicily. Decades ago. Before these places became. Before they were over.

No money. No rules. No worries.

Beach parties. High-tide parties. Sunrise parties. Dune parties.

Flip-flops on the wrong feet. Saris twisted, tripping them. Lost bikinis. Lost clothes. Lost wallets. Lost passports. Lost days and weeks and years.

One beach, another beach. Years of sand in their toes and teeth. Years of morning sunburns. Sand fleas. Driftwood scrapes. Midnight jellyfish stings. Sand in their cigarettes. In their drinks. In their suitcases and clothes.

Another glass of wine. Dizzy now, but determined.

"I wish we could do drugs. I wish drugs were still a thing," Lena says.

"Drugs are a thing."

"I wish they were our thing."

Down the path, toward the main villa—the communal pool and yet-to-open restaurant. The check-in. The concierge.

Here's the thing Lena's learned about day drinking at her age—the highs come faster, the lows as well. By the time they've doubled back to the room, two trips for things they probably don't need—by the time they've made it to the lobby, bags packed to bursting, their mood has flattened. They haven't sobered up, but the thrill is muted—the reality of trudging toward and through the sand, getting settled and comfortable, looms larger than it did back in the room.

Add to this, Drew sitting there, deep in conversation with one of the managers, who snaps to his feet at the women's appearance.

"Generation buzzkill," Hedy whispers.

Drew half rises. "Where are you two off to?"

"The beach," Lena says.

A quick glance between the two men.

"What?" Lena asks.

"It's not quite ready, madam," the manager explains.

"I told you this yesterday, Mom," Drew says.

Hedy lets her bag drop. "Isn't it born ready?"

Another shared glance with the manager. Then Drew says, "We are still sorting out a few issues."

"What kind of issues?" Lena asks.

Drew stands, as if that is that. "It's a business thing."

Another standard response Lena was used to from Stavros. As if *business* was beyond her comprehension. As if there were things she couldn't and shouldn't know.

"There are a few details that need ironing out," Drew says. "I'm taking care of it."

"We can go to any beach," Hedy says. "It doesn't have to be your beach."

"Mom, we are taking the boat to dinner tonight. There will be plenty of beach time."

"What's wrong with going now?" Hedy insists.

Lena can feel her own resistance slackening.

"We can organize a car to town for you," the manager says. "A better option in the heat of the day."

"It's perfect beach weather," Hedy says.

It will be exhausting. Soon they'll be hot and sunscreen sticky. Then the return trip. "Hedy, maybe—"

"Maybe what? Why can't we do what we want?"

The manager draws closer. He folds his hands and lowers his voice even in the absence of other guests. "We are having a problem with a small group of squatters. They've made camp on our private beach. I assure you that it's being taken care of."

"Squatters? What kind of squatters?" Lena asks.

"What does it matter?" Drew says.

"It matters," Lena says. "It matters how you treat them."

"Excuse me," Drew says. "Why are you even getting involved in this?"

"The beach is part of the hotel property, right?" Lena asks.

Drew's eyes narrow. "What does that mean?"

"It means—" Lena begins. Then holds her tongue. How much does he know about how Stavros managed squatters, interlopers, difficult tenants? Does Drew know that their family empire was built on a range of evictions, some legal and others—well, that's not for Lena to know. But she does.

"I'm telling you to be careful, Drew."

"I have no idea what you are talking about. But I'm telling you that right now the beach is off-limits and that's final."

"But tomorrow we shall have the problem cleared away," the manager says.

"Cleared? How?" Lena asks.

"How many times do I have to tell you that's not for you to worry about?" Drew says.

"Tomorrow we will be prepared for full service," the manager says.

"Thank you," Drew says.

Lena feels her shoulders relax. There's an unburdening in giving up the fight. In having the decision taken out of her hands.

"If you would like to go to town, our driver will take you to one of the quieter streets for shopping and eating," the manager says.

The town car is waiting. The interior dim and cool.

"What was that all about?" Hedy says. "You never talk back to Drew like that. You never tell him what to do."

"I was just telling him to be careful."

"You're actually worried about these squatters?"

"No," Lena says. "I'm not. I'm not worried about them."

Hedy removes her sunglasses and rubs her eyes. "Well, you don't have to worry about Drew. It's not as if he's going to get his own hands dirty."

Accidents happen, Stavros told her. Especially in SROs and tenements. Overcrowding leads to unsafe conditions leads to fires leads to disaster and casualties.

"I suppose not," Lena says. But what does it matter if you're the one who lights the match, crosses the wires, breaks the pipes? Is there any difference between that and lifting the phone, making the call, giving the order? And at the end of the day, does it matter?

Hedy removes a small tin from her bulbous purse. She opens it and hands Lena a pink capsule. "You said you wanted drugs."

"That was before."

"Take it. Psilocybin. Microdose. They relieve my ocular tension."

"Do they make you hallucinate?"

At the edges of her mind the footage of the fire destroying an entire block of downtown Los Angeles.

A building collapse in Belltown, Seattle.

"No. They make me clear." Hedy uncaps one of the complimentary bottles of water in the car and pops two pills. "Well, actually, the first time I took them, they made me trip a little," Hedy says. Then she leans back on the headrest, removes her glasses, and massages her temples. "Nothing serious though. Nothing to write home about."

Lena holds out her hand.

The driver leaves them in the historic quarter of Naxos Chora. Whitewashed homes stagger up the hillside. Marble-lined cobbled streets. Overhead a Venetian castle—signs of conquering. On a hill in the harbor, the Portara—the enormous gateway to the long-vanished temple of Apollo.

Through the winding streets.

Up crumbling staircases.

A maze of shops and cafés. Houses and hotels.

"Let's get a drink," Lena says. She's had enough of shopping to last a lifetime. Let her clothes wear in and wear out. Let them age.

"All for it," Hedy says.

They find a café—Ariadne.

Small glasses of Kitron, a local yellow liqueur. A platter of stuffed grape leaves and olives. A demi-carafe of wine.

Everything a little brighter than it should be. Everything dissolving at the edges.

Lena points to the drawing of a woman in ancient Greek dress on the menu. "She saved Theseus from the Minotaur. All it took was a ball of string."

When they were on Crete, Hedy had shown no interest in visiting Knossos—the palace where the Minotaur was trapped in his labyrinth. *Tours are for tourists*, she'd insisted.

Lena had finally convinced her too late in the day—when, sandy and tipsy, they arrived at Knossos to find they'd missed the last admission.

Look, Hedy had said, pointing over the barrier at a portion of the crumbling palace visible from the street. *You can't say you haven't seen it, right?*

Lena had hidden her disappointment that evening—well, not exactly. She'd been a little standoffish with Hedy, and a little too compliant when the Greek American gentleman had wanted to buy her a drink. A little too eager to turn her back on her friend and punish her, laugh with Stavros at Hedy's lack of culture, her disdain for museums. Then she took it too far. Quick to show Stavros her lithe figure—give him her last dance. Quick to give her life away, to prove to Hedy that she was the refined one. To double down on her mistake.

"Theseus promised to marry her, but he abandoned her here," Lena says. "She married Dionysus."

Hedy lights a cigarette. "And how did that work out for her?"

"It either killed her or made her immortal."

The street is busy with tourists and a few locals. Modern laïkó— traditional Greek music with a Western beat—pours out of open windows.

There's a shimmer in the corner of Lena's vision—a bleeding edge.

The town is bleached and blue. The walls pinked with flowers crawling upward, spreading wide.

The wine tastes of earth and sea.

"What will you do now," Hedy asks. "When you get back home?"

"You mean, what will I do without Stavros?"

"You're beautiful, Lena. But you're all dried up. We need to bring you back to life."

"I'm alive."

Hedy reaches across the table and presses a finger into Lena's sternum. "Maybe somewhere in there you are. You spend all that time doing Pilates and yoga and Aerial classes—why?"

"To stay fit."

"You're punishing yourself. You whittled away your spirit into rope and sinew draped in overpriced exercise clothes and tasteful cocktail dresses." She exhales a mouthful of smoke at Lena. "You know what you should do? Have sex. Loads and loads of sex."

Another dance long abandoned.

Especially after Drew.

Stavros had wanted another. Wanted another child like it was a decision he could make. Like he could just rent the space in Lena's body for a second kid, like she had nothing to do with it.

As far as Lena had been concerned, there was no discussion to be had. Her body. Her rules. After all, that was what she had been trained to do during all her years as a dancer. Impose limits and limitations on her body. Strangle, stifle, and restrain cravings. Deny and decide.

Drew had tested and deformed her. Made her slow and stagnant, heavy and burdened.

Stavros had badgered her, asking and asking and telling her that there was something wrong with her for not wanting a second child. And she'd withdrawn, retreating to her side of the bed, hewing to the edge of the mattress as she slept, sometimes winding up on the floor. Excuses and excuses and excuses. Hundreds of invented reasons for being unable to have a second child.

But still there were times that she had to give in and pretend.

When she stared at the ceiling, hoping it would all end quickly. After, Lena had prayed for some kind of illness to render her infertile, incapable. In the same way that in her darkest days on tour she had prayed for injury to end her dance career before the company ended it for her.

In the end it was Stavros who became infertile. Testicular cancer.

Years of anger and resentment. Years that wore Lena out as she kept up appearances, perched and chatted and wined and dined with his social set, tried so hard her limbs grew stiff and her lungs became sore from holding her breath.

t's been ages, right?" Hedy asks.

"A while," Lena says.

"That is totally unacceptable. What's the point of being rich and thin if you're all dried up inside like a cobweb?"

Hedy takes off her sunglasses and knocks back the end of her Kitron. A bit of yellow liquid clings to her lips.

Not just her lips but her eyes too. Glowing. Lena blinks the vision away.

"Nothing like a little vacation sex to get the gears turning. Stop hiding that body of yours."

Brittle. That's the word for her.

Lena exercises—diligently brutalizes herself in a constant quest for the numbness that follows the pain—when your toes are rubbed raw, blistered, bloodied, and bruised but the show must go on.

"Also, you need a hipper haircut," Hedy says. "Enough with this Park Avenue–blonde shit."

Her irises—yellower now. Not their milky blue.

"Your eyes," Lena says.

"What about them?" Hedy replaces her sunglasses.

More wine comes. The day will be wasted. Lena can feel Drew's disappointment. She will have to sleep. She will have to hide her daytime debauchery.

Now look at these young women in the town. Not dancers like Lena and Hedy had been. But lithe and supple. Stronger. Empowered with something Lena always lacked.

Young women everywhere, up and down the street. In short, white embroidered dresses—a nod to the island style. Photo polished and perfect. The right bags, the right sandals, the right hair.

"How do they do it?" Hedy says. "We were such a mess at that age."

"Being young is a profession these days. It's a job with benefits. You can monetize your youth."

"You managed that well, even back then." Hedy calls for more wine.

A group of young men passing by this time—white linen shirts open to reveal tan, muscular chests. Loose-fitting pants.

"No underwear," Hedy says.

"Hedy!"

"If you're not going to get laid on vacation, at least let me try."

"They're so young."

"Jesus fucking Christ, Lena. Not everyone has money to cushion them. Some of us need to rely on actual fun." Hedy lowers her glasses. "Sooner rather than later, I'll be totally blind. Ahead of schedule. So, excuse me if I want to see the person I'm fucking one last time."

Lena raises her glass. "To your conquests." She takes a large sip, burying her face in wine, her cheeks flushed not with shame but with jealousy. Even on the verge of lights-out, Hedy is the brighter star, the one who will most certainly get laid on this trip once she puts her mind to it.

They leave half the carafe—unthinkable decades ago—and stagger down the cobbled streets. Hedy buys an enormous floppy sun hat with *Naxos* embroidered in blue thread. Lena—a white tunic like those worn by the young women posing for pictures against the whitewashed buildings. Too youthful. Too short. But fuck it—if Hedy is going to give it a whirl, why shouldn't she? She swaps out her modest sundress.

"Look at us," Hedy says, "sexy tourists."

Lena stares at their reflection in the shop window. And for a moment they aren't there. Or they are, but it's not them. Lena peers closer at the glass. Two other women have taken their place. Younger, wilder. Strangers with hungry mouths. Demons flickering under their flesh.

A ripple of someone—something—eager to scrabble out.

She reaches for the glass. Her fingers strike the pane.

The vision is gone. It's just them—silly and middle-aged.

"Let's go," Hedy says.

It's like old times, almost. But there's an uncertainty in Hedy's step that has nothing to do with the wine. She's wary and off-balance on the cobblestones, slow-footed. She doesn't so much lean on Lena as allow Lena to guide her.

Lena chatters—commenting on the scenery, the town, some Greek graffiti. She's aware she's keeping up both sides of the conversation, commenting on the things Hedy is unable to see.

Hedy's grip tightens.

They wind down toward the harbor. Lena leading Hedy—

careful steps. Slow at times. The town grows less picturesque—more commercial. Shops filled with beach toys—pails and sieves and paddle games and rafts. Giant floaties in the shapes of dragons and unicorns and mermaids. Magnets and snow globes and shot glasses and pendants and earrings—most of which are patterned with the lapis-and-turquoise evil eye.

In the shade of the storefronts, Hedy's vision improves.

"We need these," Hedy says, grabbing two massive pendants from a booth. "Do they really work?" she asks the shopkeeper. "Can I return them if someone gives me the evil eye. If someone harms me? Can I . . . can I . . ."

She's still talking as the shopkeeper makes change, as he hands them the pendants, as they walk out of the store.

"That wasn't very reassuring," she says.

The plastic lanyard is itchy on Lena's neck. The evil eye smacks her sternum as they walk. "I have faith."

"Like you need protection," Hedy says.

"Everyone needs protection." Especially you, Lena thinks. When Hedy's sight is gone, who will help her? How will she make her way?

They pass by a boisterous restaurant—a tourist trap—that spills onto the street. They catch sight of their reflection in the plastic partition. Nothing demonic now. "We look perfect," Hedy says. "After all these years."

There's live music in the harbor. A performance at the base of the path to the Portara—the empty frame of the gate's ruin outlining the azure sky. Drums and dancing. Singing that sounds like keening, more urgent and desperate than choral.

It's a group of women. Three of them playing the drums and one on a lute or a bouzouki. Eight are dancing.

Lena and Hedy join the group of onlookers—gawkers would be more accurate.

The women range in age. Their dresses are ripped and dirty at the hems. Their hair is free and tangled. Their arms dirty. Their faces too. Some are tanned, others pale as the cold moon.

There is something wretched in the performance, untethered. The music rises and rises, like a barbershop pole, but never arrives. The dancers spin and step, twisting and twisting, out of sync with each other.

"We should dance," Lena says.

"Hell no," Hedy says.

"When was the last time—"

"I can't. Not anymore."

A coldness in Lena's stomach. Hedy unable to dance, to walk, to guide herself.

The musicians are not playing the same song, or rather not playing together. They seem unaware of one another, each turned toward her own beat.

"Looks like someone got the bad drugs," Hedy says.

Lena cannot take her eyes off the women. The dancers have let go of one another and are spreading through the crowd touching everyone, trailing their arms through the onlookers, anointing them with their music and their mania. They are different races—they even seem to be different species. Not human at all.

One stands apart from the rest. She's a little cleaner, clearer. More like an overripe party girl than a gritty hippie. She isn't dancing like the others, but conducting them with her gaze and small movements of her hands.

She might be more polished than the rest of the company, but there is still something bestial in her stare. She has the eyes of an animal.

"Imagine," Lena says.

"I can and I can't. I mean back when, maybe. I mean there was a chance this was us at one of those Goa beach parties. Just totally unhinged." Hedy takes off her sunglasses, rubs her eyes. Then shakes her head quickly, as if she can jolt her sight back into action. "We could have made a fortune," Hedy says. "Imagine us. People would have paid."

Yes—they would have. Eyes on them always. Onstage. On the beach. In the club. Everyone always watching Lena and Hedy. Devouring them.

One of the women lets out a spectacular wail—guttural and gorgeous. A sound like waves hitting rocks. Like an earthquake's roar. Lena can feel it in her stomach. She can feel it in her fingers. In her heart. She feels it emerging in her own breath.

Her arms and legs are electric.

They itch—three decades of stiffness and stagnation waiting for release.

The woman who seems to be leading the madness is in front of Lena. Black curls rising from her shoulders, flying away from her back. Eyes the color of seagrass. Glittering. A divine creature. A horrible beauty. She opens her mouth—a cry, a snarl. She reaches for Lena. Her hands claws now, her teeth bared.

A panther.

Ready to strike. To bite. To rip and rend and tear.

The scream is Lena's—terror but also joy as the woman's hands grasp her arms. She will be taken. She will be one of them.

She lets herself go—be drawn into the circle.

"Lena, no. Don't leave me."

Hedy's voice from another time, a different place. Lena couldn't reach her now even if she wanted.

Lena, flying. Lena, spinning. Lena, no longer in the harbor. No longer in the present but in—where? A cave. A temple. A ruin. Somewhere not of this time or place. A place of vines and streams and music that is inside her. Her veins are rivers. Her fingers branches. Her body more flora than fauna.

Her voice a growl.

She can feel it in her throat—a song clawing its way out.

Where is this place? Deep inside her, for sure. But also everywhere.

But there are animals there, their tongues wet and rough on her arms and legs. Their breath hot on her cheeks. Their teeth—

"Lena!"

A hand on her arm. Flesh on flesh. Clawing, scraping.

"Lena." A voice from the present.

Lena opens her eyes. When had she closed them?

Hedy is in front of her—her sunglasses discarded. Her own eyes milky and wild. Panicked. "Where did you go?"

"Nowhere. I'm right here, dancing."

"I know," Hedy says. She is breathless. "I know. I know that now. I couldn't find you."

"I'm here," Lena says. "I was always here."

"And then I found you. I felt you. But I couldn't reach you."

Lena puts a hand to her cheek. There are small scratches on her flesh.

"Do you see these?" She points them out to Hedy.

"I can't see anything at all," Hedy says.

LENA

They've dropped anchor near the beach where they will be fed grilled octopus and fresh fish baked in grape leaves.

Lena lies on the foredeck, one foot dangling toward the water. Her toes every now and then bitten by a wave.

Jordan in a sun hat, below the canopy.

Hedy sprawled out back—dead to the world until dinner.

Drew talking. Talking and talking.

"It's too big when it comes down to it and you don't really need all that space. You'll see when you get back. We're all getting used to losing him. He filled a room."

"I think I know what I need," Lena says. It *is* an adjustment though. There's more air, more room to breathe, more . . .

"With Dad's stuff gone, it will be like living in a cavern. I know you'll see. You're just not thinking properly right now. Which makes sense. It's a huge loss. And this place, I'm sure it brings it all home to you." A wave of his hand toward the beach where Stavros was found.

"I know exactly how I've been thinking," Lena says. Her thoughts are soft and floating—her daytime hangover cushioned by the pill

Hedy had given her. The evil eye hangs heavy on her neck. "You don't need to pretend to read my mind."

Drew's voice—monotone. Boring her into submission. "You prefer to stay in San Francisco, right? New York is such a mess."

In the distance drumbeats, maybe. Or perhaps an echo from the women at the harbor that's lodged itself in Lena's head. She raises a hand to her cheek, feeling the rough skin from where—what?

Drew cocks his head, alert to the music. "That noise," he mutters. "That noise." He shakes his head as if he can mute it. Then—"Mom, I found you a perfect place. Penthouse of course. New development that we're investing in. You'll love it. Attached to one of our newest luxury hotels. In the Marina. Spectacular views. All the amenities as well as the conveniences of the hotel. Everything looked after. Easy. As for New York, I'm still working on that. Maybe Brooklyn Heights. A lot going on there these days. Brooklyn. Who knew?"

"I've had enough of people telling me where to go, Drew."

"No one has told you where to go."

"What do you know about it?"

"You just followed Dad. What else would you have done?"

"Exactly. What *else* would I have done?"

She stares at her son—sees her words bounce off him.

"I'm not following you, Drew. I can make my own decisions about where I want to live."

"But there's nowhere else besides San Francisco and New York," he says.

"You have all the world's advantages, but you manage to be small-minded," Lena says.

Drew glances from Lena to where Hedy is resting. "I believe that's all the wine talking."

"You know," Jordan says, "I wouldn't mind San Francisco."

Drew moves to his wife's side. "The business is in New York. The heart of it."

"What about the tech side?" Jordan asks. "You know, with everything remote, we could. And after the baby . . ." A hand on her stomach. "It might be nice to be out of the city."

"Everything is set up for New York," Drew says. "I made the arrangements the minute we found out." This time his hand on her belly. "We'll take the Park Avenue penthouse and renovate San Francisco. Anyway, the Marina will be perfect for Mom." He lowers his voice. "Too hard to start over in a new city at her age."

"I can hear you," Lena says. "I'm not old and deaf. I'm not even old."

"I was just explaining to Jordan why we can't—"

"And why I must."

"You don't *have* to do anything," Drew says.

"According to you, we all have to do something," Jordan says.

"You'll love the place I found, Mom," Drew says. "Elegant and modern. Lively. Easy to care for."

Said as if she'd been the one caring for any of her residences in the past three decades. As if *that* had been the problem.

"Plus, Jordan will enjoy the penthouse. It's convenient for both of us."

Lena kicks the water. "I'm selling it."

Drew is on his feet. "What?"

"I'm selling it. I decided. I'm selling it and the Heights place."

"But those were Dad's." Her son—thirty years old and still a petulant child.

"They were ours. And now they are mine," Lena says.

"You can't," Drew says. "Anyway, the place I found for you is perfect. No reason to sell."

"My house, my decisions," Lena says. Salt spray hits her lips. Off-load Stavros's memory like he off-loaded a hotel that was underperforming. Off-load it like he off-loaded uncooperative tenants who wouldn't move—uncooperative squatters and the inconveniently unhoused. "Plus, Jordan doesn't really seem to want the penthouse."

"I can have you moved in before we get back to the States."

"He thinks of everything, doesn't he?" Hedy is up, unstable on unstable legs. "Don't you, Drew?"

Lena on her feet. Guiding Hedy. Bringing her to the bow.

"He really does," Jordan says. "Even things you didn't know you wanted."

"Or didn't actually want," Lena says. "His dad was like that, always improving on my wishes."

"You shouldn't have let him make so many decisions then," Jordan says.

Lena fingers her evil eye. "Well, some things you figure out too late."

"Better late than never," Hedy says.

"It's a beautiful necklace, Hedy," Jordan says. "Lena has the same. Did you purchase them today?"

"Paid a fortune," Hedy says. "Ancient magic in these."

"I thought they were tourist crap," Drew says.

Hedy takes hers off and puts it on Jordan. "Shows what you know."

"You're not really selling the houses, Mom?" Drew asks.

Jordan reaches for his arm. "Why shouldn't she?"

"I don't need them," Lena says. "I don't even like them."

"They would have made more sense if you'd had more children." A casual wave of Drew's hand, as if this subject is rightfully his.

"We had exactly enough children," Lena says.

"Did you not want more?" Jordan asks.

"Not really," Lena says.

"Did you even want one?" A curious look on Jordan's face.

"She's hardly going to admit that she didn't in front of Drew," Hedy says.

"Did you?" Jordan asks.

"Everyone wants children," Lena says.

Jordan's voice cold, clinical. "That's not true. Lots of women don't."

"Jordan gets pregnant easily," Drew says. "We'll need the space."

"Very easily," Jordan says.

Drew's hand on his wife's belly again. "Unlike you, Mom."

"You're wrong there," Lena says. Like Jordan, very easily. Before she'd even had time to think about it, there Drew was inside her. Weighing her down. If only she'd had Jordan's cold confidence back then, perhaps she could have made her own decisions.

"If it had been so easy for you, you'd have had more than one," Drew says. "Plain and simple."

"Perhaps you were more than enough," Hedy says.

"Everyone wants more than one," Drew continues. "That's going to be no problem for us. Which is why we are hanging on to the penthouse."

"My penthouse," Lena says.

Jordan stands, but Drew quickly helps her back to her seat. "Drew, honestly, let her sell if she wants to. We can quite literally live anywhere."

"That's technically incorrect, Jordan. We *could* live anywhere. But we are going to live on Park Avenue. Even you know it's perfect."

———————

They eat on an island where the coastline of Naxos is still visible. The captain points out the white buildings of the Agape Villas opposite.

Lena and Hedy wade in the warm water, their hands interlinked.

"We loved night swimming," Hedy says. "Remember Goa?"

"Remember Scheveningen?" It had been winter in the Netherlands—rain, rain, and more rain. A party in a beach club still standing out of season. High and happy they had dared each other, stripped down and raced into the gray sea.

"We could have swum to England that day."

They had felt so strong, stronger than the embrace of the sea. They could have raced the North Sea Line freighter that was pulling out of the harbor. In the water, they had barely felt the cold until voices on the shore began to call. Then the water began to bite, the current to tug them away. The sea down their throats, in their chests. They had struggled back to shore. It took them hours to shake off the chill.

"We could have," Lena agrees. "We could have made it across that channel."

What would happen if they dove in now? How far could they swim before someone called them back?

The water at their ankles. Then their calves. Then their thighs. Hedy's hand tighter in Lena's with every step. If they plunged, could Lena guide her? Could she bring Hedy to safety?

The sunset is an outrage of pink and orange—the sky on fire. The sea purple, then blue, then black. There's music from hidden speakers, Euro chillwave—safe and sanitized. Lena trails her hand in the sand, trying to remember when music had last crawled inside her, twisted and coiled until she sprang to her feet and began to release it. When the beat had replaced the blood rush in her veins, the pump of her heart. When the sound and the rhythm had been her only thoughts.

Nothing now but the canned sound of lounge beats and Drew and Jordan talking about preschools.

The caterers come with torches and when the torches burn down, they escort the party back to the boat.

The dark amplifies the sound of the waves. The sea reaches out black and lonely.

On the distant shore water ripples with light from beachfront restaurants and villas—a tease of people and company and laughter.

Down the beach, another sort of light. A bonfire. Flames leaping. Soaring skyward. The captain aims the prow straight for the conflagration.

"Is that our beach?" Jordan asks.

"Is that—?" Drew is on his feet.

"What is it?" Hedy asks.

Lena takes her hand. "There's a bonfire on the beach in front of the hotel."

Drew grips the boat's railing. "Give them a wide berth," he barks at the captain.

"Why? Who are they?" Lena asks.

"How should I know," Drew says. "Just steer clear."

"I thought you'd moved the camp," Jordan says.

Drew's hand firm on Jordan's shoulder. "Don't think about them."

"Ah, the squatters," Hedy says. "They're still here."

"Not for long," Drew says.

Lena shivers despite the warm evening air. A quick look at her son. Does he know about Stavros's policy with people like that?

Drew turns his back to the beach. "Just ignore them."

They are closer now. The captain turns the ship, heading for a small dock north of the bonfire. But they can hear it, smell it. Burning cedar. Roasting meat.

"Smells delicious," Lena says.

"Mom, we just had delicious. Actual cuisine."

"No, Drew, it really does smell wonderful," Jordan says.

Lena can hear the pregnant hunger in her voice—an overwhelming, consuming need.

The smell is divine—rich and seductive. Meat and more.

"I told you to ignore them." Drew's voice is tight and clipped.

"Because then they'll go away—if you pretend they don't exist." There's a snide leer to Hedy's words.

Jordan is on her feet now, her gaze trained on the fire. "Jordan, please," Drew says. He pulls her by the wrist, away from the boat's railing.

"Why? What's wrong with looking?"

"Do you not want them to see you?" Lena asks.

"Why would I care?" Drew says.

Jordan pulls out of his grip. "It really smells—"

"Jordan!" Drew says.

Her shoulders slump. She steps back from the railing.

"I'll have something excellent sent to the room if you're still hungry," Drew says.

The music starts when they dock. Drums and some kind of wooden flutes. Drew helps all three women off the ship. Ushers them more like. Hurries them into the waiting SUV that will whisk

them up the hill. But not before Lena sees the woman from the harbor, the panther. The conductor.

She stands apart from the fire. She waves, then beckons. *Come.*

Is it possible that Lena can hear so clearly from this distance?
Come.

The voice right up in her ear. Her chin pulsing where the
woman had bitten her. Lena puts her hand to her face. Had this
woman really bitten her?

The woman is backlit by the bonfire. A solid shadow. How is it
that Lena can see her green-glass eyes? How is it that she can feel
them watching until Lena's party is out of sight.

"Mom!" Drew's voice—the same bark he had used on Jordan.

A cord cut. The woman, vanished.

LUZ

ifty-five. I came back from the UK to Amsterdam to find the party had moved on. I know what you're thinking. Too old for clubs and beach parties. Too old for three-day festivals. Too old for staying up all night. Time to settle down. Time to get straight.

You're thinking I should have become a better mother—a grandmother in fact—because you're sure I wasn't a good one to begin with.

You're thinking I should have learned from my mistakes and my punishment.

You figured I had all that time in prison to reflect and reconsider—to make amends and make plans for a different future.

But what do you know?

Day after day inside—each brick had a name, each crack in the concrete told me a story—and the only thing I wanted to do when I got out was climb back under the night's canopy, restart the ritual and the mystery. Bend the space-time continuum. Embrace the telepathic connection born on the kaleidoscopic resonance of the dance floor.

I wanted to resume control—of you, of them, of everyone in the club, at the two-day rave, the beach party. I wanted my kingdom back. I wanted my dominion.

I wanted my subjects—some of whom were not too dissimilar to the long-haulers inside who punished me for my shorter sentence by making each day interminable.

Three years away and the whole scene had changed. People moved. Got sober. Got married. Got pregnant.

Strangers lived in my house.

My son had moved to South America. He fled after what he did. He couldn't do the time, so he chose me to do it instead.

But women—we can survive anything. We endure. Did he know that inside, the sort of men I controlled after hours would dominate and denigrate me? That I would beg from those who used to beg from me? That I would yearn for the blackout delirium that came the few times I dosed myself to the edge of death?

Did he know that the women would treat me worse?

Did he know that, nevertheless, I would emerge stronger?

I thought I had raised him right. Raised him with different rules. Raised him to respect the trade and the trade-off. But he named names—mine. And I named no one.

Three years. Time enough to plan what I would say to him. What I would do.

But he was gone when I reappeared.

I raised the monster who took me down. Or at least the one who tried.

I came back.

The music had changed. It had softened. The drugs had changed too. People had doctors. Prescriptions. Medical grade. People were microdosing. Measuring their intake. People were hiring shamans and guides to lead their trips.

The festivals had gotten even bigger, more commercial, more expensive. Destination weekends planned out years in advance. Yoga as well as drugs. Packaged experiences.

But I am used to being an exile. My parents fled Colombia for the Netherlands. (My mother—a housekeeper for a famed drug lord—had heard too much, knew too much, and was offered asylum.) I swapped school for clubs. Day for night. A job at a desk for something fiercer and wilder. I knew how to flee.

I followed the music south. Summer. Italy. Portugal. Spain. I needed to find my followers. I needed to bring them close.

The savagery of those women on the inside was burned into my brain. I held the key to their cure. Under my command, they'd reform, repent, their violence transformed and vanished. I was the one who could tame them and bring them to heel.

But I'd left them behind. I'd find others.

There's power in being wanted. In being in demand.

You need me. You give me strength.

And when you find me, I won't let you go.

discovered that there's a benefit to aging. You are more ghostly with age. More invisible. More invincible. You grow more ghostly with time. You can carry more when people look at you less.

I met the young women in the lobby of my hotel in Barcelona. They could have been anybody, interchangeable with the thousands of women I met at Dance Valley, Tomorrowland, and Awakenings.

They were on their way to Dreamwerks. They were wearing their festival clothes—halter tops and crowns. Feathers and sarongs.

They had jewels glued next to their eyes and in the middle of their foreheads. They had body glitter.

They had third eyes that could not see.

They thought they were one in a million but they were everyone I'd ever met. Their eyes were clear but would soon be shiny and vague. They were beautiful now, but their minds would exaggerate their beauty later and then they would cease to be beautiful.

They'd turn ugly and no one would notice but me.

They ignored me until they realized I had what they wanted. Then they never left me alone. They told me about the DJs. They told me about the setting. They told me I'd never see a sunrise as beautiful as the one that was coming tomorrow.

I let them talk. I let them tell me everything I already knew. I could see the future. I knew they would lose their crowns. Their halters would come untied. I knew their makeup would run. I held the key to their evening.

"Are you going to party with us, Mama?" they asked me.

"Do you like to dance?"

"Have you heard Bassjackers and Don Diablo and Agents of Time?"

"Have you been to Sonor and Futuurwerld and Untold?"

The names and places meant nothing to me because I'd seen and heard it all and you can't put a label on a feeling.

Their questions hit me like light rain. Familiar and innocuous.

We went to the event together. They seemed amused that I was game.

The main stage was enormous. An underwater theme with a giant octopus hovering over the DJ. Tentacles stretching a hundred feet in every direction—waving and releasing enormous blue-green bubbles. Traditional hallucinogenic iconography. The organizers intent on jamming a feeling into every orifice—insisting—instead of letting you come up on your own.

I'd seen it all before. The only thing that changes is the scale, bigger each year.

A few smaller stages. Still themed. Enchanted Forest. Toadstool Garden. Lunar Landscape. Same shit eternally regurgitated.

I hung with the girls for a while. I let them introduce me to their friends, their acquaintances, people they just met. I was building my web. My own tentacles going out into the party. I would draw them close and send them away. I would watch them dance as if they were dodging unseen lasers, their overflow of emotions pouring out in psychic and physical abandon. I watched them trace fractals in the air, paint pictures. I watched them try to pluck invisible objects from the strobe beams, tie the wind in knots, cocoon themselves in the music that each one was certain was for her alone.

I knew they would be mine.

A festival that size, I usually let myself sell out. A good thing, because when I returned the next day, I raised my prices, held my customers hostage. How quickly I manipulated supply and demand. How easy it was to make them want me more.

But I always saved one pill for myself. A reward for a job well done. Because I wanted to see castles in the air that are only revealed in the syncopation of the strobe lights. I wanted to feel everyone's heart beating as one—a reverb that rises from the ground up my legs and into my heart. I wanted to be the electric body and the body electric.

I wanted to dance with strangers who were momentarily my best friends. My second self. My conjoined twin.

I wanted to chase the feeling of that first high—harder and

harder with each passing party. I wanted to reignite the spark inside that was fast fading, grasp the fleeting euphoria that I've dulled over time.

Sometimes I got close but never all the way.

It wasn't long before the music was rippling goose bumps on my skin and centrifuging my chest so badly I had to open my mouth and let out some kind of primal roar. My body divided into parts— my legs and arms spasming in different rhythms, my fingers ticking on some kind of pulsing movement that seemed important and inevitable. I was lifted on a tidal wave of sound.

And I was lost.

I allowed myself to wander because I knew that I would come down and find my way home. You walk a fine line, when you're high, between losing yourself and finding everyone else. But I knew what I'd taken. I understood its contours. I knew when it was rising and when it would let me down.

I left the main stage. The crush of people. The obscene pyrotechnics.

I wandered through the smaller stages. Some too chill. Others too hardcore.

In the Enchanted Forest I caught sight of one of the young women who'd brought me tonight. Her friends were gone.

She was dancing in front of the DJ booth, her hands scratching the air as if trying to escape.

The DJ was no one I'd ever seen before. A man with golden curls. He was shirtless. He'd painted his skin gold. The flashing lights bounced off him, making him look as if he was emanating his own glow.

I blinked. I rubbed my eyes. I decided to sit before I let the drugs play tricks on me. I lay in the grass and let time do its thing—compress and expand and balloon and shrivel. And soon the sun was coming up and the women were right—it was the most beautiful sunrise I'd ever seen. But I also knew that this was a lie told to me by my own supply.

I looked back at the dance floor. The young woman was still dancing. Her hands spinning like motors. She was down on her knees. Down on the ground, she was writhing and jerking, popping and coiling herself. She was a slinky. A robot. She was a live wire. She was being electrocuted. She was the current and the conductor.

She didn't seem the type when we met—the type to lose herself, to lose her friends.

The sun was up.

And the DJ—he was still playing. Not a bead of sweat on him. Not a streak on his golden skin.

How long had I been there? Two hours? More?

The woman was spinning and spinning. The earth at her feet flying up in clumps. She was barefoot.

She was the only one left on the dance floor.

She was the only one left at the festival. But that couldn't be right. My vision had tunneled.

The festival was packing it in. Dancers streaming and staggering toward the exits. Some being carried.

But the DJ in the Enchanted Forest kept playing and the woman kept dancing. And she kept churning the earth.

He was her puppeteer. He was her conductor.

I saw blood spurting from her feet—a sprinkler spraying the grass. But she didn't notice. She kept dancing and dancing. Her feet shredding.

I rubbed my eyes because this couldn't be happening.

I saw the bones of her toes.

The DJ kept spinning. The music was unlike any I'd ever heard. Mystic and dark. Ancient tribalcore—lutes or flutes that hinted at terror lurking behind the scrim of joy.

I knew that it would never end.

I watched the DJ. He wore a half mask over his eyes—also gold. He was the architect of the woman's every move. He could make her rise and fall. He was the one summoning that cry from her throat. He was the one raising her arms into the air. He made her fingers wave and her arms rotate at impossible speed, at inhuman speed. He was the one making her spin and spin as she showered the ground with blood.

I felt the empty pill bottle in my pocket and wondered what it would take to do that.

The festival vanished around me.

I sensed the midday sun.

Maybe I had made a mistake with my own supply. Because I must have been hallucinating when I saw the woman weep blood. When I saw blood gush from her mouth. All that blood tornadoing around her as she continued to spin. A fountain. A waterwheel. Rain on a windmill.

I wanted to tell her to stop dancing but the words were beyond me. She was beyond me, out of reach. I knew that she couldn't and wouldn't listen.

The music stopped.

She fell to her knees.

I stood and left.

I am the sober one. I am the one in control. I do not let my eyes deceive me.

———————

Back at the hotel I sat by the pool. I'm always comfortable with the comedown. I rarely overindulge. I know how to ride the wave. I watched various festivalgoers negotiate the aftermath of the night. Some happy and high, some in tears. I knew they would meet at the midpoint, where there was nothing to stress over or celebrate and tonight or this afternoon they'd be back at it—another grab at the come-up.

I saw the young women from the day before.

All of them but the one I'd left with the golden DJ.

They were huddled. They were trying to make sense of something. I've seen it all before—irrationality and facts battling it out in the aftermath, rising tempers.

One shouted at the others.

They looked at me. And I pretended not to see.

Two hours later. The police gathered around the women. Real tears now. The police left.

One of the women approached me. "What did you give her?"

"Nothing that I didn't give you."

"She's in the hospital. She hasn't come down. She's unconscious."

"She'll be fine," I said.

"She doesn't know her name. She doesn't know who she is."

"She'll be fine," I said. And I knew it was a lie.

I packed my bag. Whatever the woman's fate, I couldn't have it pinned on me.

And I went ghost.

LENA

Vacation dreams hit heavy. The unfamiliar air. The exotic soundscape. All of it mixing and mingling with the everyday—tangling and tripping up the real world, ensnaring it in a web of eager delusion.

Lena dreams of dancing. The stage. A darkened theater. She knows the place—the Paramount Theatre, where the Oakland Ballet Company performed. She had danced there once—one last time after she'd moved to the Bay Area with Stavros. Or rather, she'd tried to dance. But the spirit was gone. The flow and the flex had abandoned her.

A blown audition.

A second death.

And then a month later, Drew growing inside her.

In her dream she is alone onstage, the music of the Ballets Russes' *Scheherazade* filling the empty auditorium. She is spinning—spinning, spinning, spinning. So fast she loses her footing. So fast she flies off the stage, arcing through the air. High over the orchestra. Falling fast. Readying for impact.

Lena wakes before the crash. Her limbs tingle. Her heart, on edge. Her breath tight and ragged. A sheen of sweat on her chest and back.

But still, the sound of *Scheherazade* in her ears in the darkened room of Villa Terpsichore.

Her feet touch the cool tile.

The windows are open. The curtains billowing in the night air.

Lena steps out onto the terrace. The sky is laced with stars. The pool holds their unstable reflections.

But there is music. Strings and woodwinds swelling on the wind.

She glances toward the beach. The bonfire is visible. Larger now. Rising and rising. Bringing with it the song. The fourth movement of *Scheherazade*, where the ship breaks against the cliff.

But it can't be. It must be some other music.

Lena closes her eyes. She can feel it. The ghost of her last dance lingering in her limbs and extremities.

She must follow the music.

Through the darkened villa. Through the colonnades and archways. The empty foyer.

Outside—the Agape at her back.

The music still swelling.

Her bare feet on the twisting drive. Down, down, down to the road and across. The smell of salt and char. The first sprinkle of sand between her toes. The hot crackle of the fire audible now.

Lena is on the beach before she realizes the music is nothing like *Scheherazade*. It's the same drums and flutes as when they'd docked after dinner but louder, wilder, more frantic and frenzied.

It must be the jet lag. The pill Hedy had given her. The sun and wine and disorientation of the islands. The day-for-night confusion of vacation.

This is just a bonfire.

Those are the dancers from the harbor.

And this is the beach where Stavros died. His body on the dune, close to the hotel, as if he was trying to reach safety.

There is nothing here for Lena.

Then, a hand on her arm. "You came."

The woman. The panther. The one who stood apart from the dance.

Lena flinches. Snatches back her wrist.

"I don't bite."

Lena puts her hand to her chin and feels the serrated skin.

"I have to get back," Lena says. A jerk of her head toward Agape.

"Up there? What's up there?" The woman has an accent—guttural sounds. A growl.

"A hotel. My husband's—my son's hotel."

"Not yours? Pity," the woman says. "Come."

They draw near the fire. The music feels like an earthquake in Lena's chest.

Lena catches the woman's name—Luz.

There are dancers everywhere—women. Only women. More than had been at the harbor. Their names flow in and out of her ears, inconsequential and fleeting. People she will never see or think of again.

"Dance," Luz says.

"I don't think—" Lena replies.

A quick flash of anger in the woman's eyes.

"Later," Lena says.

The encampment stretches behind the fire toward the small dunes—tents and tarps. Fabric fluttering. Wind chimes. A few smaller fires. The sticky smell of roasted meat. Laundry on the line.

Provisions tied to stakes out of the reach of scavengers. Washbasins and cookstoves.

Somewhere she thinks she hears children. Maybe hidden in the tents. Maybe kept awake by the music—their cries bouncing on the light wind.

Next to the fire, a dog is suckling her pups.

Cats as well—their poison-green eyes flickering in the firelight. Kittens probably somewhere too. A host of feral creatures on the prowl.

She's been in places like this. In Goa and Israel. In Thailand and Tulum. Off-off-the-grid. Somewhere beyond, beyond civilization.

Many of the women have fallen to the ground, overwhelmed by the dance yet still coursing with ecstatic energy.

"Where are you from? Who are you?" Lena's questions are like bullets in the air—too sharp. Too pointed.

Everywhere and everyone and everything.

We are from everywhere but now we are from here.

They are twenty women smelling of sweat and wine gathered around a bonfire. They are passing a bottle. They are smoking from a pipe that circles and circles.

One moment Lena is sitting solidly on the ground, the next her stomach has fallen away. The faces around the fire are shadow masks. Demon skulls. They are laughing.

"What?" Lena asks. "What?"

They are laughing. She smells heather and basil.

She smells something animal.

The faces around the fire, no longer human. Death masks. Disfigured in the firelight. Hungry.

Their mouths stretch and maw. Their words are savage howls.

Lena scoots back.

Their hands, claws. Reaching, reaching through the flames.

Lena can no longer hear the children's voices over the music and the fire. "Where are the children?"

"Children? What children?" Luz's voice. Normal once more. Her face and hands restored. A woman passes Lena a bottle of wine.

"I heard—"

"We have no children. Neither do you."

"My son owns the hotel. He will make you leave."

A laugh from Luz.

"He has no right to do that," Luz says, her hands on Lena's wrist, her mouth at her temple.

"But this is his beach," Lena says.

Luz fixes Lena with her panther stare. "Who told you that?"

"I heard children when I got here," Lena says.

"We never had children. Only monsters."

Through the fire, Lena sees the yawping mouth of a cave she hadn't noticed before lit from within by a flickering golden light.

Lena knows the rest of this story before it starts. How many beach parties did she attend in her youth? How many full-moon trances, raves, solstice festivals?

She might be old, but the old patterns return quick.

She accepts more wine, lusting after the bold, rich taste, far better than the curated vintages served at dinner. She slugs from the bottle, aware of the liquid dripping from her mouth, down her chin, onto her dress, golden-yellow.

A hand in hers, pulling her to her feet. The drumbeats rising from the sand into her legs, up her thighs, deep inside her stomach and heart.

She hadn't danced at her wedding or the weddings of Stavros's friends.

She hadn't wanted people to see, to judge, or to notice the flame that was dying out. She killed it before it could be extinguished by others.

A finger pressing against her stomach, as if bringing that very flame to life.

An ignition.

Then hands letting go of hers. Casting her free. She is ready.

A dervish. A whirlwind. Spinning and spinning. Stumbling like she's finding her rhythm for the first time. Her feet unsure. Her legs unstable.

The ground unreliable.

Who cares? Who cares what she looks like? How wild? How possibly deranged?

Hands on her—on her arms, on her waist, on her face. Urging her. The crush of bodies. The feel of a different heartbeat.

Fast and faster.

The beach, an indistinct blur. Waterfiregrass all at once. Faces-facesfaces. An out-of-control merry-go-round. A roller coaster shot off the tracks. Sandskysea.

One moment she is in her body and the next flung free—cast out of herself.

From a stone breakwater, a little way up the beach, Lena watches herself dance. She stands on the rocks, wind at her back, eyes on her body by the fire.

The woman she sees is a wild creature. Hands groping the night, tearing the air. Hair loose. Face stained with wine. Dress torn. Animal.

Then a voice in her ear. A man's. But unlike any voice she's ever heard before. As loud as the wind. As deep as a cavern.

A voice that seems to come from inside her. But also from behind her. It rises from the rocks at her feet. Falls from the sky above. Arrives with the kiss of the salt spray of the sea.

Faster.

Lena on the beach dances faster.

Let go.

Lena on the beach casts her arms into the air as if she's untethering herself.

Dive.

Lena on the beach dives into the sand. She writhes and wriggles, the beach her dance partner.

Now, open.

She is powerless to withstand. She has no interest in withstanding. The command is in her. It is her. It is the only thing. She feels bound to the order—as if nothing else matters and never will again.

From the rocky promontory, Lena watches hands tear at her, pulling her open.

Her heart outside her body.

Her heart in someone else's hands.

Her heart passed from woman to woman. Her pulse in their palms.

She can feel their fingers probing her ventricles and atria. Her heartbeat quickens—panic as someone squeezes too tight. A gasp. And then she feels her pulse relax as her heart is passed to a gentler set of hands.

Now set me free.

———

When she was nineteen Lena traveled with her ballet company to Prague. An understudy.

How boring to wait in the wings.

To wait in the hotel.

To wait for the call that wouldn't come.

So she'd gone out with a friend of a friend from home who had introduced her to a friend of a friend named Pavel, who'd asked her if she liked Southern Comfort who asked her if she liked dancing who asked her if she liked parties who asked her if she liked ecstasy.

And next thing she was looking at her reflection in a mirror in a bathroom in an office building she didn't remember entering—seeing a person she didn't recognize. Her but not her. She'd found Pavel in the middle of a wild party she hadn't recalled starting—DJs and trapeze artists and a light show and smoke machines—a bag of gray powder in his hand. He inhaled it in one go, his face turning red, his nose gushing with blood. Unfamiliar faces everywhere. An unfamiliar language. Out of control. Unable to communicate. To find her way out. To find her hotel.

How quickly joy turns to terror.

A knife's edge. A blade.

She'd woken in an alley. Wet. Bruised. The terror clinging to her like a new skin.

Lena cannot hear her own scream.

The man's voice again.

Set me free.

She cannot feel her racing heart. She is losing time. Everything is different now. From the promontory she cannot reach her body. She gropes the dark, not dancing. But scrabbling, scrambling desperate to climb back into herself. Trying to raise herself from the sand. Trying to become whole.

And then she is back in front of the fire. The world resettled.

A glance over her shoulder toward the water where she had just been standing.

There's no promontory.

A look around the fire.

There is no man.

Just the women around the flame, no longer dancing.

The wine continues to circulate. Lena drinks heedlessly.

"Who was that man?" she asks.

What man? What man? the women chorus. *There was no man. No men.*

"I heard a voice. A man's I think. I felt it," Lena says.

You felt it? What did you feel? How did it feel? Suddenly everyone wanting to know. All eyes on her. The women crawling closer.

The mother dog growls, warning of some unseen threat to her pups.

A movement in the dunes.

The women turn as one.

"There is always someone watching us," Luz says. "I'll get more wine." She heads for the cave.

Time. How long? A few minutes? Half an hour? Then she is back with a jug. "We steal it from the vineyard up the hill."

The liquid is cave cooled. Liquid amber. It tastes earthy. Ferrous. Lena gulps it down.

"I should get back." But back is miles away it seems. Farther than up the hill. The white linen sheets. The climate-controlled air. The marble bathrooms—a different world.

"There is no back," Luz says.

Then a cry. A shifting on the ground. The women around the fire leap to their feet.

A snake has slithered out of the dune grass—almond-eyed, sibilant. All fork-tongued flicker and sly greed. The size of Lena's leg.

One look at the circle and it heads straight for the pups.

One in its jaws.

A howl from the mother dog.

The snake has turned, making for the grasses. The mother dog leaps. The women follow.

Lena with them.

They plunge through the dune grass. A wild war cry. Lena's feet cut by the small sticks and stones. The grass grabbing her ankles. The night has teeth.

The grass, fingernails.

Everywhere a hissing.

The sky—a thousand malicious eyes.

The snake taunting, taunting them. Then in a clearing, there he is, coiled. His scales sequined in the moonlight. His eyes unblinking. Fangs, deadly glimmer. The pup still alive in his jaws.

"Aaaeeee."

The women at once. Lena too.

They pounce—a riot of limbs and hands and nails and teeth. The smell of the snake's blood. Its venom.

Teeth and fangs. The women biting. Clawing. Blood in Lena's mouth.

She sees the pup discarded to the side. She scoops it up. The snake has escaped. The women follow.

Lena cradles the pup.

The air is filled with the cries of the women in pursuit. Throaty ululations in a foreign tongue—a call-and-response with the mother dog's desperate barks.

Lena staggers back to the fire, where she collapses. In front of her, the sea. Behind, the warp and weft of the dune grass. The chase is like a wave—rising and falling with the calls of the huntresses. The grass bending and swaying.

The rescued pup crawls up Lena's chest, burrowing, looking for its mother's breast.

Needle teeth. Desperate pawing.

Lena pulls down her top. Feels the pup's hot breath. Its desperate pulling.

The fire crackles electric.

The night stills.

The grass stops its sway.

The dark swallows the women's cries and the dog ceases to bark.

The mother dog returns to the fire first. She snaps and growls as Lena disgorges the pup from her breast—hackles raised, eyes yellowed.

The women come next. Some are bloodied—black-red streaks on their fingers and cheeks. Some are bruised.

The fire falls, dwindling to coals.

LENA

Dawn breaks red and pink then yellow. Lena's eyes flutter. There is sand on her sheets. There is sand in her hair. She smells of meat and snake blood.

Can she taste its venom? Is that what lingers, bitter, on her tongue?

She puts a pillow over her face.

It's a hangover like none other. Instead of the throbbing pain she'd expected when she first cracked her eyelids, her brain is electric, alive with energy.

Still high?

Still wired?

Lena puts a hand to her heart. Its beat is steady, strong. There's something else. Bruising. Tenderness. She turns on the light, glances at her flesh. Fingerprints on her breast—deep purple smudges. As if someone had reached in—no, impossible.

There are scales under her fingernails. A shred of snakeskin on her pillow.

The sky burns, then calms, then reemerges pristine Aegean blue.

She stretches—her limbs feel powerful, taut, as if ready to dance again.

Morning has caved to afternoon. Drew will be concerned. He will be looking for her.

In the shower Lena washes the sand from her hair, the dirt from her hands. She cannot wash the scratches and bite marks from her breasts and nipples. She cannot scrub away the bruising.

She closes her eyes under the luxurious stream from the rain shower trying to recall the way her heart had beaten as it was passed around the bonfire. Red and raw, alive in everyone else's hands.

After the shower she stands naked in front of the mirror—her chest a road map of her adventures, a timeline of purple and red marks, punctures from the pup's needle teeth.

Hedy is at the door.

"I thought you had died. It's noon."

"Can't I sleep in on vacation?"

"Not if it means you're abandoning me in this mausoleum with team killjoy."

"Has Drew asked for me?"

"In fact, he hasn't."

Drew is in the lobby, too preoccupied to greet her. His father's son. He's huddled with the manager, the concierge, and two men in official uniforms—army or police.

"Drew."

Her son looks up as if he's forgotten all about her—confused and angry. An expression she recognizes from his childhood when some aspect of his day—a playdate gone wrong, a classroom injustice, an enforced bedtime—was out of his control.

"And you can't just sweep them away, clear them out?"

"It takes time," one of the officials says.

"Even after this, even after what they've done?" Drew's voice is rising in pitch—a tantrum is coming to a boil. "That beach should belong to this hotel. I've done everything to ensure that."

"Well, there are some lingering questions. But I'm sure it will be sorted out," one of the officials says.

"There is no question that those women down there are dangerous. None at all."

"Drew?" Lena says. "What's going on?" She places a hand on his arm. She can subdue him.

"You look weird, Mom."

"Good morning to you too."

"There's been a disturbance on the beach, ma'am," the concierge says.

"That's what you call it?" Drew's voice is rising again. None of his father's stoic poise. "A disturbance. Mom, those women, they chased a man through the dunes. They mutilated him."

"What?" Lena says. "What are you talking about?"

"You heard me."

There had been no man in the dunes. Only a snake. She had seen it—scaly and coiled. She had tasted its blood.

The only man, well, she couldn't call him a man at all. A feeling. A presence as powerful as the ocean, as forceful as the rock.

"Yes," Drew insists. "Oh yes. But these men won't do anything about it because *it's a delicate situation*."

"Mr. Baros, I assure you we are doing everything about it," one of the officers says. "These things take time."

"They could have killed him. The week my hotel opens," Drew says. "I want them gone."

"We are still investigating what happened," the officer says. Lena glances at his badge. *Gabris.*

"What's to investigate? There's blood on the beach. There's a wounded man in the hospital. There's a horde of filthy women camping illegally in filthy tents eating filthy animals they got who knows where a few steps away from my hotel."

"There's one man's word against the voice of twenty women," Officer Gabris says.

"So?" Drew's cheeks are flushed and flamed. "So? So? So?"

"These situations are more complicated than they appear. It is not simply a question of *removing*," Officer Gabris says. "There are governmental policies and international—"

Drew takes a step back. Lena watches him, thinking, thinking. A deep breath. "I see, of course." Another breath. "Of course. We will handle the arrangements. Not an *eviction*, that isn't what I meant. A rehoming."

Rehoming. Lena had heard the same term from Stavros. But it was a rehoming that went wrong. Or that was unwanted. That then ended in a fire, which meant some of those intended to be rehomed no longer needed homes at all.

And now the same term out of Drew's mouth. The same calculated planning. Perhaps he knows how Stavros operated or perhaps brutality is inherited. Either way, the outcome will be the same.

"Just get them off my beach. Or I'll do it myself."

"Drew," Lena says. "You'll do nothing of the sort."

"Why, Mom? Why? Why wait for them to kill someone next time?"

"They're not going to kill anyone."

He turns from the officers so he is facing Lena. He lowers his voice. "Mom—those women are camping exactly where Dad died."

"Yes," Lena says. "I can see that."

"And what? You don't think it's strange."

"Inconvenient maybe, but not strange."

He takes her by the elbow and pulls her farther from the officials. "You don't? Not even a tiny bit? Dad died on the same strip of beach where those women attacked a man."

"Your father died of a heart attack," Lena says.

"Maybe," Drew says. "But maybe not. That's what the island doctor told us. I bet he was wrong. I bet those women had something to do with it."

Lena reaches for his arm again. "That's crazy."

"Mom, they attacked someone."

"No, they didn't," Lena says. "There was no man."

He shakes free of her touch, takes a step back, anger and confusion battling it out on his face.

"It wasn't a man they were hunting. It was a snake."

"How do you know?" He narrows his eyes. "You have to be fucking kidding me."

"They chased a snake, not a man. I can show you."

He whirls her away from the group as if she's a child about to have an outburst. "You what? You can what?"

"If you want to see," Lena says.

His voice low and sinister. "We will talk about this later."

"There's nothing to talk about," Lena says.

Drew rejoins the group. "Snake or man, I cannot have a group of feral women playing huntress on my beach. I want this taken care of and I want this taken care of soon."

"As we told you," Officer Gabris says, "any situation with itiner-

ants must be handled with delicacy. But we assure you we will handle it."

"By tonight?" Drew, always pushing his luck. Always wanting
more than is on the table.

"As soon as we can."

ena can feel his fury—as if it has a body of its own. When Drew
was angry as a baby it was almost as if he doubled in size, became
uncontainable.

"I can show him," she says to Hedy. "Wait here."

Across the Agape complex and back to her room.

Her bed still unmade.

Where the shred of snakeskin had been—a single human tooth.

DREW

His father trapped his mother. That's the way the story was told behind closed doors at the Olympic Club or on the yacht. A dancer. In a foreign country. Exotic despite the fact that she was from Ohio.

There's glamour in what his father accomplished.

A real feat. Returning home from vacation with a prize.

Jordan was different. The kind of woman you earned. The kind of woman you deserved when you got a double-barreled Ivy League degree. No hunt. No chase. Just the meritocracy of like recognizing like.

Some of his friends had trophy wives. Women whose manufactured and maintained beauty masked their questionable pedigree. Women sort of like his mother but more glamorous and less refined. Not dancers, no. But certainly former party girls.

Something to look out for, his father had warned when Drew had brought home a Slovakian beauty from a Mediterranean cruise. Something you always have to watch out for. When it's in the blood, it's in the blood.

He keeps an eye on his mother at lunch on his patio. Counts her drinks. Hedy's too. You can never be too careful. Especially now that he knows where Lena went last night. How easily she slipped through his fingers. How quickly she is backsliding.

She is covered up. A modest dress. Unlike Hedy, who is overflowing her bikini top, her sarong—a mess of abundant flesh. But perhaps that's what happens when you go blind—you can't see the disorder of your own self.

"Mom, was it like the parties you used to go to? Did it make you feel young?"

Lena lowers her wineglass from her lips, looks at him over the rim.

"Was it a recently widowed thing? An impulse?"

"Was what?"

Drew stops himself from rolling his eyes. Jordan told him it makes him look juvenile. "The beach party. The bonfire."

"It wasn't really a party," Lena says.

What else could it be? A bonfire on a beach with music. "Sounds exactly like the kind of party you went to before Dad."

"How do you know what kind of parties we used to go to?" Hedy asks.

Drew feels a flush on his neck. Why must she always cut in with her questions? Why must she always challenge his reality? No, not *his* reality. Reality. Period.

"Come on," Drew says. "Everybody knows."

"Do they?" Hedy replies, draining her glass again. "I wonder how."

"It was more like a gathering. Not really a celebration." Drew can sense his mother coming around to his side. "Just, like, a hang."

"A hang? What are you now, a stoned teenager? Anyway, a

gathering with music on a beach *is* a party, Mom. That's the literal definition of a party."

"It's one definition," Hedy says.

Drew glances over at Jordan on her lounger—the barely visible swell of her belly, her sensible sun hat. A glass of ice water with rosemary. Twice as educated as Hedy and she's not nitpicking away at his truth.

He'd worried about taking her to Europe on account of their permissive approach to drinking while pregnant. But Jordan has remained solid in her refusal. It's a relief.

"But if you never really spent time partying, I guess you could see it that way," Hedy says.

"Were there drugs?"

"Drew," Lena says, "I really don't know. I don't think so."

"Until that man was attacked."

He watches Lena refill her glass. "That didn't happen. There was only a snake." She turns to Hedy. "Do you believe this? Drew thinks those women had something to do with Stavros's death."

A hideous snort from Hedy.

Drew flashes Jordan an imploring look. Could she please cut in with something sensible and save him from this nonsense.

"It's a theory," Drew says.

"Why would they want to kill Stavros?" Hedy asks.

Drew grips his wineglass. Why the fuck did his dad have to locate this damn hotel near some ancient mystic ruin? Why couldn't he have made it easy for once? So much fucking red tape just to set up a row of beach chairs.

"Because they are on drugs," Drew says. "You'd still recognize drugs, right, Mom?"

Another ugly laugh from Hedy.

"I mean—how many times would you say you've done them in the past?"

"Some things you can't count," Hedy says.

"Maybe *you've* lost count. But I was asking my mother."

"What does it matter, Drew?" Lena says. "What's the difference if it was twenty times or a thousand?"

"Numbers matter, Mom. Analysis. Prediction. The more drugs you did in the past, the greater likelihood you'll do them in the future." Everyone always arguing with basic facts.

"I'm not sure that's accurate," Lena says. "Ask a recovered addict."

"I don't have to," Drew says. "Actions. Numbers. Patterns. It's basic business."

He watches his mother sip her wine. How many glasses now?

"I'm a person, not a pattern," she says.

"I need to estimate the probability of a regression."

Lena lowers her sunglasses. Are her eyes red? Are they swollen? "Regression? Drew, really." His mother hides her eyes before he can get a closer look.

"I'm just trying to get a sense of what I'm dealing with here."

"You're *dealing* with your mother."

"A side of her I didn't know," Drew says. "It's going to take some getting used to. One moment your mother is a poised socialite, the next she's raving on a beach. Forgive me for being the rational one."

"I wasn't raving. God, what a word."

"Antiquated," Hedy says with that ugly laugh again. She sounds like a drowning horse.

"Mom," Drew says, "let's not split hairs. What kind of drugs?"

"I really don't know," Lena says. "I already told you. I didn't see any."

"You don't know what they were or you didn't see them? Which one is it, Mom?"

How infuriating can one woman be?

"Okay, fine, Drew. They were smoking something. I don't know what. And there was wine. Satisfied?"

"I won't be satisfied until those people aren't just gone but off this island." He refills his glass, checks that Jordan is still sticking to water. "And I won't be satisfied until you promise me you won't go back there. That you'll stay by the hotel."

"I'm not promising anything," Lena says. "This is my trip too. My vacation."

"This is not a *vacation*. It's a business trip."

"A family business trip," Hedy says.

"It's my business and my hotel," Drew says. How come this needs to be explained? "That campsite will be cleared by tomorrow evening." He feels less certain than he sounds. Because there are loose ends. Issues about cultural preservation. Some rubble in a cave that archaeologists claim was part of a shrine to some barely known god two bazillion years ago.

The crap he has to put up with.

"But the officers said—" His mother always with the objection. Always piping up like a first-year law student.

"They said what they said, but they didn't say that I can't take care of it myself. Problem, action, result. Business 101."

"Drew, really. There could be children there."

"Even worse."

"You cannot seriously be thinking of evicting children," Lena says.

Jordan shifts on her lounger, clearly bored by this pointless argument.

"How can you be sure of what's there and what isn't, Mom?"

"What do you mean?" Lena says.

"He means you were too high to know what's what," Hedy says.

Lena puts down her glass. She stands and smooths her dress. "As if you know anything about being high, Drew. As if you have the first clue about what I can and can't remember."

"Drew." Jordan is on her feet. She's at his side. She's got his back against his mother and her ludicrous friend.

"Imagine, Jordan. Can you? Imagine what it was like down there."

"I can't," Jordan says. "But perhaps a more diplomatic approach."

"We don't have time for that," Drew says.

"A discussion," Jordan says.

"Mom, in your opinion, do you think a *discussion* with these women would be productive?"

"No," Lena says.

"See, Jordan. I appreciate that you're being levelheaded but my mother says they are too unhinged to see reason."

"That's not what she said," Jordan says.

"A discussion with them won't be productive because they have no desire to leave," Lena says.

"If you know so much about them, Mom, you tell them to go. You clean up this mess."

"It will only be a mess if you make one," Hedy says.

Drew doesn't even look her way. She's the real mess here. A disabled freeloader full of ideas.

"I could use a nap," Lena says.

"I bet you could," Drew says, glad to see her stand up from the table. Off the women go, Lena looping her arm through Hedy's. The blind leading the blind.

———

When they are gone it feels as if someone has turned off irritating background music, the kind of stuff you hear in big-box stores. The cheery noise meant to distract shoppers from price tags and fool them into loading their carts with crap they don't need.

He exhales and leads Jordan back to the cool sitting area of their suite.

He's got people on the case—a team of historians ready to invalidate the archaeologists' claim that there's anything of note down on that beach. And when they do, the beach is the Agape's—his—free and clear and those women won't stand a chance.

He puts a hand on Jordan's stomach.

His father always said there are things you make and things you build. People admire the things you build but it's the things you make that are your greatest achievement.

This baby and the ones to follow. A real family. The first of many ways he will outperform his father. Too bad Stavros won't be around to see.

Jordan brushes his hand away. A brisk gesture.

"What?"

"Nothing. It just feels weird."

"Weird?" This is not a Jordan word. She speaks with the arrogant precision of her international upbringing.

"I'm fine. It's just your hand, right there."

Hormones and travel and stress. Not to mention his mother's lunacy and her lunatic friend. Not to mention that band of lunatics down on the beach. Everything set up to destabilize his stable wife.

"But you *feel* okay?" Drew says. He puts his hand back where it had been. "Everything *feels* normal?"

"I guess," Jordan says. "I've never done this before." She moves to the couch, props her legs on the coffee table. "I don't want to assume."

Cautious. Drew likes that. Not jumping to conclusions or raising the alarm.

But still, *weird*?

"Can you be clearer?"

"I don't think so," Jordan says.

"We can't find the solution unless we understand the problem."

"I didn't say there was a problem. I said it felt weird." Her tone placid, matter-of-fact, something Drew usually admires when it's turned on one of her clients or a less educated acquaintance. But now.

She begins leafing through the Assouline coffee table book Drew had commissioned fabricating the history of Agape—a collaboration between a famous travel writer, a local poet, and an award-winning photographer.

Jordan's mood makes sense. Drew has heard stories from his friends whose wives bristled at their pregnancies. All that work they put into their bodies. All those hours at the gym and time spent logging calories and hiring trainers and trying new diets. Then a shift. An imperative that you can't control.

The infinity pool sloshes and slaps.

Too loud?

A cloud passes over the pristine sky.

The room is shadowed. Suddenly too dark.

Drew glances at the control panel on the wall. He'll have to do something about this, reprogram the lighting. He presses the button to call the manager.

He's no nepo-heir to his father's business. He knows the trade. He studied negotiation, executive speaking, and business impact. While his classmates were starting hedge funds and disrupting tech, he took online hospitality classes in hotel management at a no-name college in the Midwest. Sure, he could have gone into private equity and VC, raiding and restructuring floundering hotel chains. But Drew wanted the family empire. He wanted to be ready.

People think he's finicky, spoiled, to the penthouse born. But he loves the details. He loves making things click and tick. He loves polishing and perfecting and the thrill of launching a complete project—the arc from developmental planning to initial marketing and operations.

He loves the feeling of being a puppeteer, a conductor, bringing a whole business into concert and making it sing. He knows the rack rate, the RevPAR, and how to predict the occupancy forecast. He knows how to balance functionality, luxury, and profit. He knows the art of the upsell to those who can't afford it. He knows the importance of room fragrance, unisex bath products that make men and women alike feel pampered and sexy. He understands that the whole hotel has to tell a story, not just be a place to stay.

So don't call him spoiled or demanding. Luxury isn't just an experience. It's a business and a science. The hotel isn't just a hotel. It's a curated experience with a thoughtfully crafted and entirely fictitious backstory that informs all the details—a tale of a widowed shipping magnate who built a palace to his beloved wife. Despite this, the margins are slim and the place has to sell out in the high season.

Drew stares past the curtains to the patio. The sky is stormy. The room really is too dark for midday. Another problem, but also an escape from the larger problem of the women on the beach and the women in this hotel.

The door to the suite opens.

The manager at last.

He should knock. Drew makes a note.

The air shifts. A smell that shouldn't be there.

Drew feels a prickle on his skin. A seasick sway in his stomach. He's unsteady on his feet.

A woman darkens the door.

How can he smell her from here? Brine and wet wood shavings. Her black hair falls halfway down her back. Ovular green eyes. Olive skin.

His mouth opens, then snaps shut. The words won't come.

"Who the fuck am I?" Her voice is guttural. "That's what you want to know?"

Her eyes—they are glowing. They are making Drew dizzy. But he can't look away.

"I think you already know. You tried to ignore us last night. But we saw you. We felt you intruding on our beach."

He can feel Jordan bristle. "Isn't it the hotel's beach?" she asks.

The woman takes her eyes off Drew. "Is that what he told you?"

He feels his speech return. "How the fuck did you get in here?"

"Nobody stopped me."

There's no security in place yet. Only the high-tech system that puts the rooms on lockdown but doesn't prevent people coming through the front door. No thought to keeping outsiders and trespassers from the hotel because until that moment Drew—no, not just Drew, everyone—had assumed the Agape's forbidding luxury would be security enough.

Another problem to solve. Another protocol to put in place.

His fingers reach for the phone.

"What will that accomplish?" the woman says.

"You need to leave," Drew says.

"My friends and I don't appreciate you sending police to clear us from the beach."

"I don't appreciate you depreciating the value of our hotel with your campsite."

"I would be careful, if I were you." She steps toward him.

She seems to grow as she draws closer. Her presence fills the room. *Be very careful.*

Did she speak those words?

The beach isn't yours, is it?

Drew glances at Jordan. She doesn't seem to have heard the woman's words.

"Or what," Drew says. "Or you'll attack me like you attacked that man last night?"

"Your mother knows there was no man."

"Stay away from my mother."

"She's the one who came to us," the woman says.

"What the fuck did you bitches do to her?"

A whole semester's class in effective speech and communication strategies and Drew knows he sounds like a dick. His father and his accent—always laying it on thick with plumbers and drivers and repairmen, any working-class person who crossed his path. Always playing the part of the son of the immigrant cabdriver. Well, it's not Drew's fault that he doesn't have that luxury.

Bitches?

Her voice in his head again. Under his skin.

"You should leave us alone."

"Get out." There's a quaver in Drew's voice that he hates.

You shouldn't order me.

"You're trespassing." He points toward the door. "Get out of my hotel."

She doesn't move.

"And get off that beach. You have no right to live there."

"Who says?"

Eminent domain. Squatters' rights. Drew has heard enough of these things to last him two more lifetimes in the hotel business. Hurdles and hoops that can and must be jumped through with money and more money and a gold standard PR team. And if that doesn't work, there are other ways. "And my father has owned this property for years."

"We have a spiritual connection to that beach."

"Don't start with that," Drew says. "I don't want to hear this shit about some crumbling temple."

"What temple?" Jordan's voice—cool but curious.

"It's nonsense," Drew said. "Just some stupid nonsense."

Is it?

That voice again.

You aren't exactly sure, are you?

"Shut up!" Drew feels the red flush in his cheeks.

"Who are you talking to?" Jordan asks.

He points at the woman.

"Why don't you come see for yourself what is on the beach before you decide to kick us off again?"

"So you can do to me what you did to my father?"

The woman holds his gaze. What is he seeing in her eyes? His father dead on that beach. Dead near these women. Dead because of them.

"What are you afraid of? A few women?"

"You killed him."

"Drew." Jordan again, trying to pull him back.

The woman looks over his shoulder at Jordan.

Drew wants to protect Jordan from this woman. He wants to drag this woman from the room, but something prevents him from touching her. From approaching her.

"What about you?" the woman asks Jordan. "Why don't you come?"

"That is the last thing she's going to do," Drew says.

The woman sidesteps him, closer to Jordan now. "You don't have anything to say?"

"I'm thinking," Jordan says.

Then the woman is at Jordan's side, her hand on Jordan's stomach where Drew's hand had been a few minutes ago.

"There's a monster inside of you."

Jordan's eyes lock on hers.

"We grow the monsters that take us down."

Jordan freezes. Not thinking clearly enough to pull away.

"Monster?" Jordan asks.

"I birthed the son who imprisoned me."

Drew can't touch the woman but he can touch his wife. He pulls her to her feet. "Go to the bedroom. I'll take care of this."

A startled look on Jordan's face. Her eyes grazing where his hand holds her wrist.

"They are all monsters," the woman says. "But come and see and I will show you how to defeat them."

"Let go," Jordan says, trying to pull free.

Footsteps. The slam of a door.

The woman is gone.

Drew pursues her down the hall. Through the courtyards. Into the lobby and over to the concierge. But she's too fast.

He returns to the room where Jordan sits, a stricken look on her face, her hands clasped over her stomach in pain.

A storm comes out of nowhere. The sky is thunderous and the pool is pelted with rain. Surely they can predict the weather better than this. They eat dinner indoors in Drew's suite.

Jordan is pale. She picks at her salad. Her stomach cramping.

Phone calls to doctors back in the States. A local doctor on call.

No bleeding. Probably nothing to worry about. Hopefully psychosomatic, although he wishes Jordan were above susceptibility to mind games.

"What's wrong?" Lena asks.

Jordan's hand on her stomach.

"It's your fault," Drew says. A furious glance at his mother. "One of your beach friends came here. She—" She what? *Cursed Jordan. Touched her.* Neither of these words does justice to the violation.

"She told me there's a monster inside me," Jordan says.

"And you believe her?" Lena says.

"Of course not," Drew says.

Shock. Coincidence. Stress—all valid reasons for the pain in Jordan's stomach.

"No," Jordan says. "Not really."

Not really. Is everyone losing their fucking mind?

"Not *not really.* Not at all," Drew says.

But what is it at the back of his mind? What is that twinge of uncertainty? What if?

"I saw her too." They all turn to Hedy, who has been unusually silent through dinner. "I saw her when she came in."

"You did?" Pointless of him to even bother asking why Hedy hadn't stopped her, why Hedy hadn't said anything.

"She touched my face. She told me she could make me see."

A tidal wave of relief. Just fucking nonsense. All of it. Because there's no way, none.

Drew laughs. "Well, that's not fucking happening."

He refills his glass. A big sip. The red wine running through him.

Soon all of this will be back under his control.

BEFORE

saw him again at Trance World.

I saw him at Solar.

BaXXus—a perfect name. Divine and druggy.

I kept my distance. I'm not part of the cult of the DJ. I've seen too many women lost in that game, hanging around and around, hoping and hoping, and ingesting more and more to stay up late and later in order to hope some more.

They forget that I am the one who has what they need. When he stops playing, when he stops paying attention to them, I'll be there.

You can't chase a guy who's always going to run away to the next festival, whose job it is to trick you out of yourself with music, who wants to make you lose yourself. Who will leave you in his wake.

I know because it's my job to do the same. But I never play you or abandon you. Because I need you as much as you need me.

I watched him from a distance. He played tribal house. Complex drum patterns and percussive chants in languages I'd never heard before. It was dark, aggressive. Pots-and-pans noise. Ululations that sounded like screams.

He played darkside. Darkcore.

He looped screams. He spun terror riffs.

It was a familiar soundscape until it wasn't. It lured you with something familiar—the promise of a build to a higher plateau. A sonic elevator that raised tension and raised the flesh on your arms and neck. It built and built, summoning you to the peak where it should have exploded into all-out euphoria, milked the release into a rushy-gushy drop in which you were free to loose your caged emotions onto the floor in wild relief.

But that release didn't come. BaXXus took you somewhere darker. The buildup didn't empty out onto the top floor of carnal release. The drop never came. Instead, he brought you down into a new tunnel—a scary sonic maze of labyrinthine sounds, cries and screams that chased you through electro corridors searching for a way out and a way up, separating you from the rest of your tribe, who had started the climb with you.

And then the climb began again.

And again.

Torturing and teasing but never setting you free.

I watched him work the dance floor until the women around him collapsed. I watched him dance them raw, golden sweat dripping from below his mask and beading on his already golden chest. He was tall, muscular. Always bare chested. I watched the women fall. I watched them stand and return for more. I watched them dance until they bled.

I wanted to do what he did. Because around him, they had less use for me. One pill and they were his. Sometimes not even one.

Festival after festival he worked them ragged. Danced them to the brink, to the precipice.

I saw them in the aftermath. I saw them at the hotel, the beach, or the airport, depending. I saw their altered faces long after the drugs had worn off—a change both subtle and unmistakable. They glowed. They glistened. They longed and craved.

They wanted him more.

They wanted me less.

And that I couldn't stand.

They followed him. An entourage. A clique.

I saw them on the Balearic Islands. I saw them in Romania. I saw them in Croatia and Sardinia.

They had left their families, their homes. They no longer wore festival clothes. They wore rags, handmade garments. They were barefoot. Sometimes they begged.

They slept on the grass. In the sand. They slept under the stars.

They were his and his alone.

They turned their backs on me.

I was on the beach. Portugal but it didn't really matter. It could have been anywhere. The parties were interchangeable. High-priced hedonism. Aural and visual smorgasbords. Bodies and sweat.

It was the day after the festival.

I was at a beach club—palapas and beds on the sand. Café del Mar playing in the background. A smooth comedown aided by over-priced rosé.

I watched the sunset.

I watched the night rise from the sea to the sky. In two days I would move on—a different island, a new party. The same circuit over and over until fall, when I would vacation somewhere far from the music and mayhem.

I took my drink to the water's edge. The sea was high-summer warm. The water caught the reflection of the lights from the beach club, sending golden ripples from my toes.

I walked through the water—the liquid cooling the last hypersensitive nerves on my skin, bringing me back down.

Up the beach was a steep dune. From the dune a different kind of music—singing. I turned from the water.

The moon had risen and hung bright and low like a spotlight. So bright it cast a shadow.

I watched the dune, trying to figure out who was singing.

Then I saw them—the women who followed BaXXus. They came sprinting down the hill and headed for the water. One of them knocked the glass out of my hand.

They were a wave, sweeping past me. They toppled me to the ground.

They plunged into the water. And in the sea, they glowed gold.

I returned to the water's edge and watched them swim, their tattered dresses trailing around them as they lit up the waves with their golden light. They swam far from shore—farther than I thought was safe. But who am I to judge safety? I am the one who pushes you to your limits and beyond. I am the one who will inspire you to jump off the deck of a yacht in the middle of the ocean in the middle of the night. I am the one who sets you free.

I watched them disappear under the small waves. A minute. Two minutes. Three.

And before I had time to taste the fear that was rising into my mouth, they were back. They emerged from the ocean reborn, their dresses transparent and soaked. Their hair plastered and their eyes glowing in the moonlight. They were luminous. They were tall, strong. They were more than they had been when I first encountered them.

I tried to remember when I had seen each of them before—at which festival had each appeared for the first time? When had they joined this strange band?

What had they taken? What were they taking? What was BaXXus giving them?

Thirty years in my trade and I know my products, their effects and side effects and aftermaths.

These women were a mystery.

In prison they had ways of controlling us. Dehumanizing methods of coercion. Sexual. Transactional. Behind closed doors, behind barbed wire—no one cares.

Always a trade for our humanity.

The guards had our fate in their hands, their fingers in our souls. They could reach deep inside us and make us do things we'd never do outside. Never do in our right minds.

They took advantage of our desperation to debase us.

It came down to a question of survival. A job for your shadow-self.

It's the same thing you tell yourselves the morning after. That it wasn't you kissing and groping and stripping yourself bare.

It wasn't you writhing in the sand, on the dance floor, eyes and hands and mouths on your skin.

It wasn't you telling everyone your secrets.

Turning yourself inside out.

Giving yourself away.

wondered what part of these women I was seeing now. How deep inside them had BaXXus reached? How much had he removed? What had he left behind?

I stepped to the side to let them cross the wet sand.

The moon was higher now, over the sand instead of the ocean. The women clasped hands—a string of twelve across. They looked up at the sky. Or so I thought.

I followed their gaze, wondering if they were going to howl at the moon. But then I saw him—BaXXus standing on top of the dune. He was golden. Brighter than his followers. Brighter than the moon.

He was there and he was gone.

The women screamed and gave chase. I watched them race from the beach into the dunes, baying, braying, wild and untethered.

I listened until their cries died away.

I was angry at how he controlled them. I was angry at how well he did it.

No man would be my boss.

No man would dig deep into my flesh, my soul, and manipulate me.

But me—I'd do those things to others. After all, it's my job.

've witnessed collective mania before. I know there's a dark side to the dance—that people become fixated, frozen, their minds looped and looping. That they unhinge themselves, get lost. They burn hot and burn out. Make choices that they can't unmake. That the euphoria becomes slippery, fleeting. Slimmer and thinner with more darkness than light. That chasing it becomes a compulsion.

I wondered how long these women had before they flamed to dust.

How long could he keep them afloat?

One more drink before heading back to my hotel. Anonymous. A late-middle-aged woman on a lonely vacation. Nothing to look at.

But then I heard them again. Their cries louder. A stampeding down the beach.

A wild boar charged past. I could feel its terror. Spraying its pig sweat.

The women in pursuit. They brought the animal to the ground. They tackled it. Sand and bristles flying.

A noise from the beast unlike anything I'd heard before. A near-human scream of terror. One of the women pulled back from the boar. Blood dripped down her chin. Her mouth filled with fur.

The animal was still howling as they ripped its flesh.

Broke its limbs.

It was screaming as they ate it.

The air smelled of gore. Intestines seeping into the sand. The night hot with blood.

Collective mania—it's not just a party thing. I saw it on the inside too. A chance grudge, a communal hatred turned on a newcomer, someone who exuded frailty or was frozen in terror.

I've seen women pounce and devour—cull the weak.

I've witnessed feral unrestraint that left bloodstains on the already bloodstained walls.

I didn't imagine it existed on the outside.

The women's mouths were painted red with the boar's blood as if they were the ones who had been slaughtered.

Their teeth glowed.

Their eyes were the size of the moon.

The sound of ripping flesh. The crunch of jaws. The crack of bone.

I felt someone watching me from up on the dune. But I did not look. I know better than to fall under a spell.

I've already mentioned, I am beyond manipulation. I did my time.

But his eyes bored into me, filling me with golden light I could sense but not see.

Turn. Turn.

I did not turn. No man will tell me what to do.

I put my hands on my back where I could feel the twin columns of his gaze. My skin was warm. I imagined that it glowed.

Turn. Turn.

His voice in my ear although he was far away. His voice in my head. In my lungs. In my limbs. On my breath.

Turn. Turn.

I wanted to turn. Instead, I walked away, the scent of death still in my nose, the hunger to do what he did in my heart.

JORDAN

Monster.

It's what her mother had called her. *Monster. Monstrous.* As if it was Jordan's fault for being born. *Little devil.*

Demon.

Whispered in her ear at bedtime when she couldn't sleep. Snapped across the dining room table when she spilled her food.

Jordan hiding under her own bed, convinced that the monster she feared was really her. Convinced she was destructive. Violent. Poisonous to others.

Jordan in her closet.

Jordan locked in the bathroom.

Jordan begging and begging to be sent away to school, where she tried to see that it was her mother who was the monster.

Primary school. Secondary school. University. Postgraduate. Twenty years of achieving and overachieving. A promise never to make the mistake her mother had—marry her way up in the world as if that was a solution. Lena's mistake too. But at least Lena loved Drew in her own sappy, doting way.

Jordan would earn her place. Choose her husband. Plan for a child in her own time should she want one.

Do what educated, professional women had earned the right to do.

Make her own choices. Guide her own life.

You'll see, her mother whispered in her ear at the wedding.

You'll see, her mother hissed into the phone when Jordan told her she was pregnant.

"See what?" Jordan had asked. But what was the point? Her mother, a miserable bitch to start with, had evolved into an even more miserable drunk. And that too was Jordan's fault.

B ut now. The word. That hand on her belly, summoning the fear—the knowledge—that Jordan had suppressed, ascribed to her mother's instability. The monster conceived out of apathy. Out of anger. Out of a lack of desire for what was growing inside.

It's fed by reticence.

By fear and hatred.

I t's already in her.

Just like it was in her mother.

Feeding off her hesitation. Her uncertainty and ambivalence.

And now it will grow.

The more Jordan thinks about it, the more weight and reso-nance she gives to the idea—the more certain she becomes about the creature inside her.

It can hear her thoughts.

Her doubts nourish it.

Each hesitation, each worry making it more grotesque.

How had the woman known? What had she seen?

Where is it written? On her face? In her eyes?

Is it too late?

LENA

She cannot sleep. Not insomnia. Not jet lag. Something else. Energy. Excitement.

All day, when she should have been bone-tired, when her senses should have been dull and her thoughts dragging on account of too much wine and too little sleep, she had been alert. Not just alert—awake. All the brittle tension in her body crumbled—her limbs loosened.

She could feel the blood in her veins.

She could taste the air. Hear the grass.

When the storm broke across the sky, she could feel the raindrops in her chest, the thunder in her heart. It shook her from the inside out.

And now in bed, her body feels electric. As if the lightning was lingering in her limbs.

She keeps the patio doors wide open. The storm has blown away. She can feel the night. She can feel its breath. Its animal-hot heat. She feels it wrap around her, pulling her to her feet.

"Lena."

And now her name.

"Lena."

The voice is Hedy's. Lena fumbles for the light.

Hedy is standing at the foot of her bed. Lena blinks, her eyes adjusting.

"What are you doing?"

"Your patio doors were wide open."

Hedy's dressed as if she's heading out for the evening. She's wearing rectangular black sunglasses with ornate gold plastic arms.

"Are you going somewhere?" Lena asks.

"Take me to the beach," Hedy says.

"No. No way."

"Lena, please."

It should be enough to stay here, enjoy the kind of comfort of which most people only dream. "No." But the air is delicious—tempting. It wraps its fingers around Lena's wrists, pulling her into a sitting position.

"Because of Drew?" Hedy's voice, hard. The same firm disapproval Lena had heard three decades ago on Crete when she explained she was going out to dinner with Stavros instead of to a beach club with Hedy.

"Let's just keep the peace," Lena says. "It's not that difficult."

"Now that your husband is dead, you're going to let your son tell you what to do? I thought you were stronger than that."

"You've always been the strong one, Hedy." Lena flops back on the bed.

Hedy reaches out. "Please."

"I'm tired."

"No, you're wide awake. You weren't even sleeping."

"It's not a good idea."

Hedy laughs so loudly Lena imagines the sound disrupts the infinity pool.

"How much time do we have left for bad ideas? I told you what that woman said to me. I told you what she promised." She removes her dark glasses, bugs her eyes wide at Lena. "Look. Look before there's nothing left to see."

Her eyes are wild, struggling to focus. She waves her hand toward the bed. "I want to see you and I can't."

"Hedy—"

"I want to see perfectly again. Even if it's only briefly and in the dark."

"She didn't mean it," Lena says. "Or she meant it metaphorically."

"She told Jordan there was a monster growing inside her. And if she's pregnant with your son's kid, there's nothing metaphorical about that." Hedy replaces her glasses. "Fine," she says. She turns, her hands in front of her, feeling her way out of the bedroom.

"Where are you going?"

"I already told you. To the beach."

"In the dark?"

"Lena, for me it's always dark."

The thought of Hedy on the twisting drive from the Agape to the road. The thought of her crossing the road to the beach blind. The thought of oncoming cars. The thought of her staggering across the sand. A misstep. The water instead of the shore. The thought of her being swept away.

"I'm coming," Lena says.

———

She glances over her shoulder as they pass through the lobby—alert for the sound of someone coming to stop them. She expects to hear her name, to be recalled and restrained.

"You're acting as if we're a couple of teenagers sneaking out of the house," Hedy says. "But you're a grown-ass woman leaving a hotel she goddamn owns."

The lobby is silent.

Without guests, there is no one on duty. The heavy wooden door clicks shut behind them.

Down the driveway—the landscaped lupines and poppies rustling in the night wind. The manicured olive trees, silver in the moonlight.

Across the road.

The air growing briny.

The sea silver-black.

A cloud across the moon, darkening the water. Then clear again.

Down the beach the bonfire's flicker—its roar inaudible at this distance. Dancers circle the flames, magic-lantern silhouettes.

Lena pulls back on Hedy's hand, stopping them in their tracks. "Are you sure?"

"Why? What?"

How to explain that with the joy had come terror? How to tell Hedy that she had stepped so far outside herself she'd lost track of her own body. Her escape so utter and complete she'd seen her heart passed from hand to hand. She had heard a man's voice in her ear, felt him so close, inside and on top of her—part of her. His breath in her veins. His blood in her heart.

Fear and anticipation. Two sides of the same coin, flipping wildly and never falling.

Lena puts her free hand to her heart. Checking. She feels it beat. She feels the surrounding bruising.

"Come on." Hedy tugging on Lena's hand, pulling her across the beach. "I smell the fire."

Lena follows, half leading, half keeping pace. A messy, ungainly approach. They stumble, kicking sand. They lose their shoes.

From a distance she can tell that there is a larger group around the bonfire tonight. They come closer.

Lena sees the same faces as last night but there are now younger women in the mix. Better dressed. Fashionable. Vacation clothes. Vacationers. Their eyes wide and wild and wondering. Their mouths open and ecstatic. They dance too close to the fire. Skirts on fire. A flaming Tilt-A-Whirl.

This newer group separates from the others. They circle Lena and Hedy. Their words a jumble of languages and utterances. Growls and nonsense.

Their mouths snarl.

Lips licked.

In the firelight, Lena can see scratches and scrapes on their tanned flesh. She can see the blood on their mouths.

Hedy removes her glasses, squints, puts them back on, trying to bring the scene into focus.

The young women swarm Lena and Hedy. Pressing in tight and tighter, pulling at their clothes and their hair. Bringing them down to the sand.

"Lena!"

Hedy's voice panicked. Her hand grasping for Lena's. Slipping through her grip.

The women on top of them. Breath and nails and teeth.

Blinded by hair. The smell of others in Lena's nose, their taste in her mouth.

Fingers in her ears and eyes.

Teeth on her neck.

"Lena!" Hedy's voice muffled this time.

And then the crowd parts. The women retreat.

Luz is standing over them. She holds out a hand to Hedy, pulls her to her feet.

Hedy fumbles on the sand for her glasses. Lena finds them, shattered. "Sorry," she says, extending the broken offering.

Luz takes them from Lena and tosses them away. "She won't need these." She turns to the young women. "Behave, you savages." Her tone sneering, dismissive. "Go dance," she says. "Dance and be free. Dance until the night tells you its secrets."

The young women stare at Lena and Hedy—their vision suddenly clearer. Then, like a pack of shamed dogs, they slink to the far side of the fire, cutting their eyes at Lena. Their tongues still flickering over their lips.

"Come," Luz says to Hedy. "I will fulfill my promise."

A worried look at Lena.

"She will be fine with me," Luz says. She holds out a bottle of wine to Lena, who drinks and then passes it to Hedy.

The wine hits warm and electric and smooths Lena's rough edges. The scene around the fire changes. The young women no longer snarl. Their faces relax. They are loose and limber.

Lena watches Luz lead Hedy away. She watches her friend disappear into the mouth of the cave.

She's been taken.

Whyherwhyherwhyher?

Luckyluckylucky.

The younger women stare after Hedy.

Where is she going?

What's in there?

Lena drinks more and the music starts and time unspools and stops and rewinds and ceases to matter.

Luz returns from the cave, extends her hands, raises Lena to her feet.

"Last night I saw them rip my heart out. And I heard a man's voice. Controlling me."

"Nonsense," Luz says. "There are no men here."

The women—the vacationers and the squatters—have assembled around Lena and Luz.

Lena feels something inside her—something rising. A snake that's twisting, slithering through her insides. Limb to limb. Down her spine.

She feels it writhing past her liver. Coiling around her heart.

She watches her limbs wave and sway at its passage, her knees buckling.

She feels it rise from her toes up to her neck.

She opens her mouth and watches the snake emerge from her lips, fall into the fire, and turn to dust.

Then it is just her and her now electric body spasming and coiling with the sense memory of the serpent that she released. The dance it left behind.

Lena cannot stop.

Her body is not her own.

The women surge closer.

They want to touch her. They want to become her.

Their hands running down her arms. Her cheeks. Her legs.

They want to know what is inside her.

They are stripping her. Pulling her dress away. Her underwear. Their fingers everywhere.

Lena feels the moonlight silver on her skin.

She feels dozens of fingers stippling her flesh.

Deeper into the dance. The night pulling back. The fire receding. The tide taking the water away.

The women are touching her. Raking their hands down her limbs.

Lena watches her flesh come away in strips. She sees the pink muscle of her forearm. The web of veins and arteries.

They peel off her thighs, discarding the skin in the sand.

They strip her back like a hide, flaying her. The air feels different now—racing through her exposed organs. She feels everything and too much. Each grain of sand kicked up from the beach. Each air current.

She watches the blood and bones of her fingers weaving the air.

She watches the muscles on her feet carving the sand.

She watches her blood flow from her heart and return.

She watches the ballooning of her lungs.

They peel away her cheeks, her chin, and her nose.

She feels the breeze in her eyeballs, in her eye cavities, in the holes where her ears used to be. The night rushes in. It becomes her breath. It moves her body.

What won't you let us see?

Nothing. Nothing. Nothing.

Her flesh is gone. The women trample the strips of skin into the beach.

She is raw muscle.

She is cord and tendon. She is the essence of the dance.

How much time has passed? How much has she lost?

Lena is naked by the fire.

Where is Hedy?

Lena is surrounded by conversations that go nowhere. Women kissing and groping one another. Women naked in the sand, in the sea.

Where is Hedy?

Here is Luz raising Lena to her feet.

"I know you. I know women like you."

"Where's Hedy?" Lena asks.

"You think you've overcome the madness. That you've tamed it. Inside you are all wild creatures."

"Where's Hedy?"

"Your son is going to try and banish us. But he won't succeed."

The reality of the beach solidifies around Lena—the squatters, the looming hotel. All the recent magic gone and evaporated. "He will," Lena says. "That's what he does. He succeeds."

"He shouldn't even try," Luz says.

Lena knows that she will lose more time and space. Lose distance and connection. She knows the faces will darken and grow monstrous. She knows there will be menace in the grass, poison in the sea, death in the dark. It will be real and unreal, beautiful and terrifying.

And before it happens—before a new delusion takes her—she needs to find Hedy.

Walking is harder now. The sand cratered with unseen depths that swallow her steps. The air unstable. Lena holds out her hands as she circles the fire searching all faces for Hedy's. They wear masks. They wear smiles and grimaces. They show teeth and tongue. Lips and spit.

Away from the fire. Toward the cave.

No one needs to tell her she shouldn't enter.

A smell from the mouth—earth and iron, blood and wine. Rotten and divine. Lena breathes deeply—her thoughts dragged from the beach to the airport. The same scent emanating from the women deplaning from Naxos.

And now a howl. A grunt, a groan of pleasure shaking the cave, rattling its firmament, raining silt down to the floor.

There, in the middle, a golden lion—its muscled back to Lena. A crown of ivy in its mane.

Below it, Hedy, pinned to the earth.

The lion gives off a glow, enough to light the cave.

Lena can see Hedy's eyes wide and focused, fixed on the beast. There is blood on her lips, smeared across a delirious smile. Her legs are wide.

I want to see the person I'm fucking one last time.

A roar from the beast. The cave shakes. Hedy's eyes wider, so wide they look as if they might pop. The tendons on her neck ready to burst. A noise coming from her throat that Lena has never heard before. A noise that is not human. Not terrestrial.

Hedy's head pivots. Her eyes move from the lion's face to the cave's mouth. Her eyes on Lena.

"Lena!"

The flash of recognition. Her vision clear.

The lion turns, fixing Lena with its deadly amber stare.

Help me.

Is that Hedy? Is it the beast?

Lena takes a step forward.

Another growl.

And then black.

HEDY

I n the cave there is a man I cannot see but I can feel. When he breathes, the walls shake. The floor rumbles with his heartbeat.

How do I know? I just know.

I know that I want him without seeing him.

"He will make you see," the woman says to me. She lets go of my hand and urges me forward. "If you believe. He is yours. You can do what you want with him."

She presses a hand to his lips. Then she leaves.

Oh boy, do I believe. If I didn't believe, I'd have nothing left but my darkening world.

My vision, reduced to two pinpricks, is like seeing the world through a straw. I can only take him in in pieces. A puzzle I have to assemble. Gladly.

I hold out my hands.

Long hair. Muscles. So many muscles. Goddamn, do I want to run my hands down those arms and down his chest.

A man for me. Just for me.

But there's a chain. It rattles when he lifts his arms.

Open your eyes.

"They are open."

He gives off a golden glow. I feel it warm on my skin.

I run my hands over his chest. There are two slits on his ribs. My hands come away sticky. Blood. I lift my fingers to my lips. His blood tastes of honey.

Now open your eyes.

He is radiant. More energy than human. A force.

Set me free.

Why would I do that? I need him, here and now and trapped for me. I need him to make me see.

I want him more than I wanted to be the best dancer. I want him more than the thrill I got from performing. I want him more than all the drugs I'd taken to distract myself from my impending blindness.

I want him with a fury that I've never experienced before.

I feel his heart in my chest.

I lick his wounds. I can hear my own hunger.

The chains rattle.

I feel almost godlike as his blood slides down my throat.

In my mind, he is no man but a lion. And with a roar he is on top of me.

Open your eyes.

There is a universe on the roof of the cave. There are stars. Constellations so fine and clear I could connect the dots with a pencil.

And then there is the man himself. So golden and radiant that I cannot see the details of his face. But I can absorb him—a cosmic energy that feels as if it might shatter me.

Open your eyes.

How much wider can they go?

Insects and raindrops and the fine lines on my knuckles.

Lena's eyelashes. Her crow's-feet.

Lena is here. Her bug-wide eyes. High on something. The revolution of her eyeballs. The needlepoint of her pupils.

Her naked body. The whiteness of her flesh. Stripes of blood on her arms and legs.

Has she come to take this man from me?

Lena who can have anything. Who has had everything, here and naked.

"Lena," I shout. The word comes out different.

Then I see the look on her face deforming her over-elegant cheekbones. Revulsion. Horror. As if what I'm doing is dirty. As if she wouldn't dare.

Go.

Does the man say it or do I?

Her hand over her mouth. Stricken. Stumbling backward.

I'm sweat-slicked, aware of each droplet as it rolls down my temple, down my back, down my thighs. I stand. The cave comes to me in perfect detail.

I see columns that were not there before.

A shrine.

A small temple carved into the wall.

I'm aware of every crevice. The dome of the ceiling. The way it tapers toward the floor. I see how the salt water has stained the rock walls. I see the dust of trampled seashells. I see the man collapsed on the floor, his chained arms above his head. His wounds leaking golden blood.

He is beautiful and monstrous, deadly and divine.

And he has made me see.

For the first time in decades I see everything. But it is too much. Too clear.

I can pick out each strand of hair in his curls. I can follow the network of veins beneath the skin of his forearms. I see the blood flowing toward his heart and back.

At the mouth of the cave, I see the beach and the sea.

In the fire, I can make out the core of each flame, the shape of each wisp of smoke.

And now I am aware of the eye color of every woman still transported by their wild dance. There's blood on their cuticles and wine staining their ragged, chewed lips.

It's too much.

Each blade of dune grass—the fresh and the dried.

The universe beyond the stars.

The craters on the fingernail moon and the tease of sun on the horizon.

The beginning and ending of everything all at once.

I see and see and see until I can't bear to see anymore.

BEFORE

I have witnessed eight overdoses firsthand, six fatal. I won't tell you how many of those were a result of my own product.

I sell clean stuff. But I can't control what you do with it. I can't control if you mix it with cheap shit. If you have a heart condition. If you're dehydrated. If you have weakened yourself to the point that just a taste more is what breaks you.

But still. Those are the moments you need to walk away. Take a breath. Take a break.

You probably think I have blood on my hands.

And maybe.

Those women with the boar. That was blood on a whole different level. But it wasn't the blood that bothered me. It was the man who held their strings. Who commanded them. Who summoned that mania and bloodlust.

I had to keep away.

I know all about temptation.

In Mykonos I crashed in the guesthouse of a villa owned by a man who sat way higher up the food chain than I—who had fingers in Afghanistan, Morocco—who imported and exported in dangerous waters.

After the boar, I pivoted from festivals to the yacht circuit. Fewer customers but higher prices and demand.

That season I watched heiresses lick orange life preservers. I watched princes and princesses try to enter restaurants naked. I watched all sorts of extravagant nonsense—champagne Jacuzzis, daylight orgies, whole nightclubs rented for a group of four.

I kept away from parties. I wanted to put a buffer between me and what I had witnessed in Portugal.

It infected my dreams. It played in my head in daylight hours.

Their bloodlust. His power.

But still, BaXXus's voice whispered in my head. It called me back.

Another beach club. Another chillwave soundtrack as well as the slap-slap of the small waves and the ambient conversation floating through the air.

I stared at the sky.

There was an exhaustion in me I hadn't known before. I felt hollow, raw—as if I'd given too much of myself away. I was empty. I knew the high wouldn't come no matter how hard I chased.

So many faces and places and parties. So many days that didn't end and nights that were one long week.

So much of everyone else and so little of me.

The music changed. Less chill and more groovy. A slight trance beat.

I rose and dusted the sand from my legs.

The club was a labyrinth of pools and swim-up bars. Dining areas. Conversation pits. And a dance floor. Palm trees and palapas. All the usual shit.

Another drink and then back to the guesthouse.

And then . . . ?

That morning I had looked in the mirror and seen the years carved into my face. I had seen a map of my excess. I had seen the hollows in my eyes. I had seen all these things but I had barely recognized myself.

An old woman looked back at me.

Worn.

Desiccated and weathered.

I crossed the dance floor where no one was dancing. It wasn't that kind of night. It wasn't that kind of music.

There was an unfamiliar weight in my chest. I felt burdened and saggy.

Aged.

And then something inside me I hadn't felt since my early days. That first flutter—that tingle. The sense that something was going to happen.

The feeling I'd been chasing for years and worried I'd never find again because I was going dead inside. Here it was.

A spark. A glow. A radiation.

Flashback. Aftershocks. It's no secret that by anyone else's standards I've pretty much burned my brains out, depleted my serotonin.

That I'm fried and frizzled. You probably think a little high-wire activity in my nervous system is no big deal.

But this was a feeling so familiar.

The first hint of the greatest come-up. The tease of a secret that's waiting on the other side. A promise.

The notion that my heart would liquefy and flow into my limbs.

But I was sober. Mostly. A little wine and whatever lingered in my bloodstream from the weekend. Nothing that would summon this sensation.

I should have moved on. Let it go.

But intoxication is intoxicating.

We are all chasing that original, virginal experience. The one that ushered us into the scene, the one that changed, transformed, and reprogrammed us. The one that taught us that no matter what happened, we would never fully come down.

I felt it as I crossed the dance floor. I lingered and it was too late.

I looked at the DJ and only then did I notice his golden skin. I couldn't look away.

He was spinning but I could feel his fingers in my heart. I could feel him reaching deep inside me, pulling me close.

I was inches from the DJ booth. There were no boundaries. No borders. No barriers between things. No barrier between me and BaXXus.

His music was inside me. An energetic, orgiastic flow. A life-stream.

It was the pumping of my blood. The sway of my limbs. The ecstatic staccato of my breath.

I knew I could not survive without it.

I was desirous and furious at the same time.

He had trapped me.

I had let it happen. I craved it and I hated it.

I hated him for what he could do.

And I wanted to do it.

It wasn't just his music. It was him. He had flowed into me—his arms in place of my arms, his eyes in place of my eyes. I saw the world gold. I saw the beginning and the end of everything. I saw a seed, a sprout, a plant, and a barren branch.

I saw the animals behind the human masks.

I felt the moon rise in my gut.

My fingers could reach every star.

The universe was inside me. It was growing and growing. I had no choice but to cut myself loose. Let go. Fly away. And I fell.

I could not feel my body.

And then I felt it coming apart.

I watched myself splinter. I sensed my mind fragment.

I heard myself scream as I flew into pieces.

Stop.

Was that my voice? Did it come from me?

Did I have a voice anymore? Or was there only him?

Because he was everywhere inside my mind. Wherever I ran, he found me. He was down every tunnel. Around every bend. His body gold and monstrous—enormous and inescapable. A terror. An infection.

I tried to run. But I tripped on ribbons of time and sound, music dark and ancient that he'd unspooled around me. He trapped me in threads of noise, luring me down darker corridors until I knew—I knew—I would never escape. Everywhere I turned, there he was, sometimes a panther, sometimes a lion. Sometimes wielding a large stick with which he'd strike the ground and compel me to dance.

So I danced.

I danced across the sand. Through caves. I danced in darkness. I danced in a deep cocoon from which I thought I would never emerge.

I danced even though I didn't want to. Even though I willed my limbs to stop. Even though I ached and ached and could sense my feet blistering, then bleeding.

He danced me out of myself.

He danced me into exhaustion. Into terror.

I danced until there was no me. Only him.

I woke on the ground, on a blanket. I sensed fire burning some-where close by. The smell of sweat and breath. I was shaking. My limbs sore. My feet cut and bloody.

Of course I've lost time before. Too many pills and the world goes from too much color to blackout black. Awake but unaware. Stories about what you did told to you later. A night you can piece back together.

This was different.

There would be no story because there had been no me.

A woman was stroking my hair. I sat up and scurried away. I'm not the cuddle-puddle type. I've never been one for the universal love, gooey mess of emotions.

"Where?" I began. But I knew.

I was in their camp. The wild women who followed this golden man.

It was up a hill overlooking the beach. What beach and where and how far had I come—all a mystery.

I stood.

The women were gathered around the fire. Some were sprawled on the ground. Some were crawling. Some dancing. Most of them—all of them—high.

Here's a secret that you probably know.

We tell you that the drugs will set you free, but they will also make you a prisoner. Our prisoner.

I knew the hunger in their eyes. The devotion.

I also remembered what they were capable of.

I stood and walked closer to the fire. Except it wasn't a fire at all. The flickering light was coming from the golden man who reclined on the grass. The women swarmed around him like koi, circling and circling. Slithering. Starving.

They crawled close to him on either side. And they pressed their tongues to his glistening flesh. They licked and lapped, drinking his sweat, then retreated, eyes wide and wild.

I heard his voice inside me. And my heart stopped cold.

Once again, he spoke to me without speaking.

Come.

I stepped forward although I didn't want to because I remembered the chase—him around every corner, in every recess of my mind.

The women parted for me as if he had told them to.

Drink.

Another step. I felt my knees giving way, buckling, ready to bring me to the ground.

I felt my tongue tingle.

I felt my need.

My eyes widened. My heart was his.

I saw myself reflected in his eyes. And then I saw my own hunger, my need. And it pulled me back.

Let me tell you about the look in my eye. It's the same one that's on your face when you show up at my doorstep at 4 a.m. It's on your face when I'm an hour late because I had other calls and you thought I wasn't coming. It's on your face when you see the other partyers dialing in something that you worry is out of your reach.

You would think I would thrill to that look, that it would mean I have you in my power.

But it disgusts me. It reminds me that you are beneath me and I must keep you down.

The man's eyes were mirrors. Golden ponds.

I saw myself. In my eyes in his eyes, I remembered that I am the architect of the night, not its captive.

I saw the look in my eyes, and it repelled me. I fell backward, trying to hide from myself—shield myself from what I was about to become.

He noticed my resistance. He propped himself up on his elbows, scattering the women from his sides.

No?

"Who are you?"

Drink.

"What did you give me?"

Drink and you will understand.

I could feel the last hours wearing off. A comedown unlike any I had ever experienced. A sense that I would forever be locked away from my real self unless I drank.

I felt as if I was falling. Dropping from a cliff into a bottomless ocean. I lost my breath. I choked.

Drink.

"No."

I know the art of the deal. How to apply pressure if necessary to up the sale. How to give someone a taste to get them to come back again and again.

You want what I have.

I laughed. He was right but not how he imagined. "I have what I need."

You don't have them. A glance at the women.

He knew.

Drink.

I thought of the trip he had taken me on—a ride that these women never got off. The delirium was so tempting I could taste it. I could feel it.

But joy and terror are two sides of the same story.

I could see the look—my look—reflected in his eyes. I could see my hunger. My need.

I backed away. The women closed ranks around him.

I sat on the ground. After a while a woman slunk over to me. Her mouth glistened with golden sweat.

"What is he giving you?" I asked. "What are you all taking?"

Her voice was a thousand miles away. "Nothing. We have no need for chemicals. We stay pure. It's his way."

"You mean—?"

"It's him. Only him."

"His sweat?"

Her eyes bugged with desire.

I reached into my pocket for my pills. "I have something better. Something you can control." I rattled the bottle.

"Never," she said. "I would never. That's vulgar."

"But," I said, "you're on something. You're taking something."

Her laugh was bitter and angry and dismissive. "You know nothing."

"Sweetheart," I said, "I know everything there is to know about this except how he is doing it."

"You know nothing," she said.

"You all need to sober up."

"Tomorrow he is taking us to his ancestral homeland. To the site of his greatest mysteries."

"Where's that?"

"Naxos," she said, pointing across the sea.

I returned to the villa. I typed *Naxos, ancestral*, into my phone.

There was a single answer.

Dionysus.

LENA

There is sand in her mouth. At the corners of her eyes. Under her fingernails.

And now a man's voice speaking first Greek, then English.

He claps his hands and Lena bolts up from the ground as if on cue.

She's naked, covered in scrapes and scratches. She's bleeding in places—sand in the open wounds. She runs her hands over her flesh, shocked that it's all back in place. She scours the beach with her eyes, looking for any strips of missing skin.

Standing over her is Officer Gabris—heavy-browed, dark-eyed. Behind him, the hotel concierge.

Both men look at her and then look away as if she is shameful.

The concierge takes off his blazer and offers it to Lena.

She tosses the garment aside. She wants to feel the air and the salt and the sand and the lingering smoke. She rakes her arm as if she can pull back her skin.

The men step back as if she's a wild animal.

The officer clears his throat. "Up. Up," he says. "You have thirty-six hours to clear this site."

Around her is the conventional carnage of any old beach party. The bodies of the young vacationers scattered across the sand. Some tangled together. One or two women who forgot to sleep, still huddled by the fire sipping the dregs of the wine. A few, like Lena, are naked. The rest, half clothed. They yawn. They return to earth.

Lena can see them trying to dial in their circumstances—how and why they are on the beach. These are not the women who live in the camp, but the ones from town, women who are clearly tourists, vacationers.

Some of them stand and rearrange their disheveled dresses or quickly cover themselves. A few stagger away in silence.

Lena closes her eyes, drunk on the sun's warmth. Who was that woman who would have been ashamed to be found in her state—dirty and half drunk, her clothes askew, the remnants of last night's party painted on her face? How had she crawled inside Lena's skin or covered Lena with her brittle exoskeleton? Where had she come from? What demon had summoned her and allowed the real Lena to become possessed?

She's gone now, Lena knows. Stripped away with her skinsuit last night. Cast to the beach and trampled. Swept out to sea. So let the men see the disorder of her. Let them witness the wild abandon, glimpse the meat of her thighs and the ferocious power in her gaze. Let them see deep inside her. Confront what they fear. Let them bear witness.

The officer claps his hands again. "This is a private beach. If you do not clear these tents by tomorrow afternoon, we will clear them ourselves."

A rustle from one of the tents and Luz emerges, no sign of the late night or the revelry on her face.

"We won't be leaving," she says.

"Mr. Baros has arranged for alternate accommodation for you."

"We will not be confined to camps."

"A hotel—"

"No hotels," Luz says. "Or any of the other holding pens you think might suit us."

"This is private—"

"We have a spiritual connection to this beach. So we will stay."

"I'm afraid that's not your choice," the officer says.

"It is our choice," Luz says.

"You have thirty-six hours. Then we will move you."

"Try," she says. "Just try."

Lena rises. Let them see her nakedness. The concierge has retrieved his jacket and holds it out like a shield. Lena swats it away.

The thin scrim of a leotard. Nude tights. The cut and curve of her sanitized by fabric.

What's the point? The dance was her body. So let them see her body. The scratches and scrapes. The sags and stretch marks.

Onstage or at the club everyone stared, trying, Lena imagined, to see beneath her clothes. But now the men look away—the police officer and the concierge. She sees their corded necks, craning in a different direction as if by ignoring her she might cease to be.

As she climbs the dune, she feels someone watching her.

Lena shades her eyes, looks up toward the road—the brilliant white of the Agape against the blue sky.

There is Drew—the hotel at his back.

Unlike her escorts, he does not look away from her naked body. Instead, he stares and stares, a look of utter disgust on his face.

DREW

Disaster can be useful. It can make people see clearly. Bring a project to its lowest point, and the naysayers will get on board quick and understand the need for turnaround.

Problem. Analysis. Action. How many times does he have to say it?

Nothing inspires teamwork more than the threat of failure.

Sometimes the best course of leadership is to let others make mistakes so that they understand your plan of action is the right one.

A shame his mother had to expose herself in order for the police to understand the threat on the beach. But making people see clearly often comes with collateral damage.

And sometimes you have to inflict that damage yourself. He knows the dirty side of the business. But it won't come to that now.

Drew doesn't have to explain the potential fallout to the Naxos authorities. It doesn't take someone in the travel industry to see that a bunch of squatters corrupting wealthy vacationers isn't good for the island's image. Naxos has so far been spared the difficult optics refugees have brought to islands in the Eastern Aegean where tourists frolic in the same waters where migrants drown. It seems safe to say that everyone wants to preserve the island's untarnished reputation as a safe place to escape the cares of the world.

To hell with the possible ruin of a temple—some inconsequential holy site. If the rubble is the sort of place that leads to the madness strewn before him on the sand, there's no doubt the island will side with him over the nutjob historians and classicists.

He watches his mother cross the sand. For years, Drew has admired her dedication to health and fitness. Her restraint when it comes to most indulgences. She looks good in her tasteful clothes—never ostentatious, never underdressed. Sheath dresses that suggest her toned physique. Nude high heels that elongate her lightly muscled quads.

He had no idea that what's beneath the surface of those designer dresses is so—aged. It's a shame that all those Pilates and Spin and silks classes cannot fix the march of time. His mother is lean, but loose. Ropy. Flesh sagging in the wrong places.

Drew knows all about marketing—about how to sell a business hotel near a man-made lagoon as "resort-style." He knows how to cross-brand a too-small hotel as "boutique." And he knows that regardless of how many social media posts tell you that fifty is the new twenty, it's a lie. No matter how many voices in that particular aphoristic chorus—life does *not* begin at fifty. Fifty is squarely middle-aged. Fifty—older in Lena's case—has no business at all-night bonfire parties. Fifty cannot be naked on the beach. In fact, fifty should only be naked behind closed doors.

But as Drew knows, sometimes you have to let people wallow in their poor choices.

So he doesn't take his eyes off his mother.

He wants her to see him watching, see herself reflected in his confirmation of her mistakes. You lead by example. You lead by confronting problems, by boundary setting, by avoiding threat lockdown.

Drew knows, as Lena draws near, her body scraped and bloodied, her hair knotted and her eyes bloodshot, that this will be the end of it. She is devastated and destroyed. She is naked and shattered. She has been shamed. Just the way the police officer and the concierge won't look at her should be confirmation enough.

But he will look. He will look and make her see him seeing. He will watch her with the tolerant forgiveness of a son who will accept his mother's mistakes. Who will make them right for her. Because it is in his power to do so.

No more beach bacchanals. He has won.

Lena reaches the road. She pauses in front of him, as if she wants him to take a good look.

Up close the night's damage is worse. Hard to look at almost. Lena is ripped and raw—her skin shredded in places. Bruising on her collarbones. Fingerprints pressed into her neck. Her arms look clawed.

Drew waits for her to stumble. To collapse.

Her mouth opens. Her lips are cracked.

She reaches a hand toward him. Her fingers chewed. Blood ringed around her cuticles.

He is ready to catch her and take her back inside and hide her away.

"Mom?"

Lena doesn't fall. She doesn't stumble.

She grows. It must be a trick of the late-morning light. Her muscles ripple, like there's a current inside her.

"Mom?"

She is larger. Something in her eyes Drew has never seen before. The whites are amber. Her hand reaches his arm. Clasps his wrist.

How many times has his mother touched him? Thousands? Tens of thousands? He knows the feel of her hands. The firmness of her grip. Her strong, thin fingers. The softness of her palm.

There is something in Lena's hand he has never felt before.

Power.

It feels as if she might crush his wrist.

Her eyes on his. As if she can burn a hole into him. Drew wants to look away. But he can't.

The pressure of each of her fingers, digging into the fine bones of his wrist. As if she wants to snap them.

A roar. That's the sound that comes from his mother's mouth. A roar as her eyes widen—showing him their golden fire. A creature ready to pounce. Teeth and saliva and the stench of fresh-killed prey.

Drew leaps back.

Lena loosens her grip.

"Hello, Drew," she says. Her voice normal. Back to her regular size. Her slightly loose skin on her toned body scraped raw.

The breath is high and tight in Drew's chest. There's sweat on his neck and brow.

"Are you okay?" Lena asks.

Drew flaps his hand at the concierge and takes the jacket the man is carrying. He throws it over Lena, hiding her from his own eyes.

He doesn't want to see what she is now or was a moment ago.

Without a word, he escorts his mother up to the hotel. He ushers her to her room. He orders breakfast and a flight of fresh juices. Later he will organize spa treatments for her. A massage and a hairdresser. Bring her back down to earth. Clean her up. Make her normal and presentable.

Tonight is the first night that the twenty-four-hour concierge will be on duty. Drew makes a note to have her inform him if his mother leaves her room.

Now that this problem is settled, there is work to do.

Three days until the grand opening and the music in the lobby isn't quite right. Too lulling, too calm. A sense of stupor instead of serenity. The art program of local painters is missing two key pieces—one for the lobby and one for the bar. The final shipment of luxury toiletries is missing the body lotion. And the circadian lighting in the lobby goes dark too early.

Drew doesn't love the glasses chosen for the welcome cocktails. Too clunky.

He doesn't love the scent of the towels. Floral not herbal.

The in-room coffee offerings aren't authentically Greek.

The menu of experiences and excursions needs to be enhanced to include both sailing and yachting. They have to reimagine the aestheticians' outfits so they look less like doctors and more like ancient herbalists.

And he needs to test the emergency security system, should the hotel have to be put into lockdown at a moment's notice.

———

At breakfast, it is a relief to be alone with Jordan. A relief for Jordan too, Drew imagines. The chaos of Lena and Hedy and their antics haven't given Jordan the space to recover from the pain in her stomach.

She describes it as cramping. As if something is squeezing her.

Another visit from a local doctor yielded nothing beyond the platitudes about "stress of travel" and "hormones," which Drew knows is ridiculous because Jordan is one of those down-to-earth, competent women who is unaffected by the collective hysteria of trendy diagnoses.

"God what a shitshow. Those fucking women," Drew says. Because this is their fault of course. Before that madwoman and her merry band of dirty deviants, his wife had been stable, rational. But now . . .

He looks at his arm. There are bruises from his mother's touch. He yanks down the sleeve of his linen shirt, buttons it tight at the wrist, adjusts the cuff.

The breakfast table is set for two. The weather is perfect. His concerns about the noise of the infinity pool were unwarranted. Three more days and they will open with a party for influencers and a junket for travel writers. Everyone treated to a free stay. No reason for complaints. By the time the first paying guests arrive with their complicated needs, Drew and Jordan will be back in New York City.

And the beach will be cleared.

He has his mother to thank for that.

Can't have a bunch of naked women passed out in public. Regardless of cultural preservation or whatever.

"I've offered them a low-cost family hotel in the harbor. They'll have two weeks there. Then it's someone else's problem."

"And they'll go?" A frown from Jordan.

She should back him up. She should share his confidence. "They should."

"It's a shame all of this couldn't have been taken care of well before you open," she says.

"I'm sorry that in the chaos of my father's death on a remote fucking island in Greece I didn't think to ask if he'd chosen to build his hotel over a beach with a contested historical ruin."

"So it's really there?"

"Yes. No. It doesn't matter." Drew pauses, looks at his wife. There's a strain on her face he's never seen before. "Are you siding with them?"

"I'm just looking at it from both sides. If they have a claim—"

"Well, *they* don't have a claim. Regardless of whether or not there's a worthwhile ruin down there, those women have no right to be terrorizing that beach. My father *died* down there. Don't tell me it wasn't their fault."

"I really don't know," Jordan says. Always too rational. Always too levelheaded. Why can't she rise to the fucking occasion for once?

"I'm giving them a good deal. An out before they do more damage. Listen"—he reaches for Jordan's hand—"you know how this goes. We put on a good face, act magnanimous. We both know they don't want to be rehomed. Which means they will leave the cheapo hotel sooner rather than later. But at least we put on a show." He takes a deep breath. "We've been through this in downtown Seattle and the Bowery with the homeless population. We move them off our street and into temporary accommodation. Before the week is up, most of them have disappeared." He slugs his wine. "People don't want to be helped. Surely you've read about the fallacy of the NGO model. You go to East Africa, tell people to burn their poisonous khat fields, and show them how to farm and irrigate instead. By the time you're back home, all the agricultural infrastructure you've put in place is up in smoke to make way for a fresh crop of khat."

"Do you know anything about these women?"

"No, but it doesn't matter because the knee-jerk reaction to outside assistance is always the same. Which is why it's unrealistic to make any long-term commitments. What I'm doing is helping them realize that their best course of action is to return to one of the islands with preexisting infrastructure for their circumstances." He takes a large sip of wine. And another. "End of the day, they have no more right to the beach than I do."

"Which means you also don't have a right to it."

"Jordan!" Drew slams his glass onto the table, sloshing wine up his arm. "You're the stable one. The grounded one. I have enough shit going on with those damn women and my mother and her crazy friend, without you piling on. You need to be on my side. You need to back me up."

He wipes the wine from his wrist. It's still throbbing from the bone bruise inflicted by his mother.

"I'm just asking questions," Jordan says.

"Jesus. I've had enough of questions. From the manager. From the designer and the architect. From the goddamn police who want to know *why* it's so goddamn urgent to get those goddamn creatures off my beach." But she's sown the doubt, then watered it. He doesn't have this situation under control.

"I wonder," Jordan says, "why that woman from the beach said there was a monster inside me. I wonder if it could possibly be true."

LENA

S he wakes without having slept. More like coming out of a trance. But last night clings to her. Or rather, last night is still inside her.

Naked. Her serrated flesh sprawled on top of the sheets. Lena runs a hand down the claw marks on her forearm, opening the skin wider, her fingers digging underneath the too-protective shell. Peeling it back. Trying to tease out the self who had danced on the beach—the real Lena inside her skinsuit.

Deeper and deeper until the blood runs over the thousand-thread-count sheets.

Blood on her fingers.

Blood in her nail beds.

On her palms.

She looks as if she's been savaged by a wild beast. By a lion.

But—but that wasn't her. That was Hedy.

Hedy.

Lena bolts up in bed. Where is Hedy?

She had woken up on the beach alone. She had walked alone

across the sand, up the dunes. She had stood alone in front of Drew and alone she had allowed him to escort her to the hotel and to her room.

Lena grabs a robe. She glimpses herself in the mirror as she runs from the bedroom.

A wild woman. A beautiful creature. She glows gold. She is taller. Stronger it seems. She has taken a new form.

Someone has been in her room to deliver breakfast. The table is set. The doors to the patio are open and the breeze sweeps the curtains inward. The infinity pool continues its unceasing fall.

Lena lets the door bang behind her. Her robe is improperly tied. Her body revealed in flashes as she runs across the Agape toward Hedy's room.

Runs? Flies is more like it. Whatever magic, manic energy filled her last night, still coursing through her limbs.

"Hedy!"

Her fist on the door.

"Hedy!"

She could break through. The wood, no match for her hand.

"Hedy!"

No answer. No answer. No answer.

Back down the landscaped pathways, the fresh air electric on her raw skin.

Into the main building, where more employees have appeared since yesterday. A woman at the concierge desk.

"Madam," she says, stepping from her post. "Madam."

"My friend," Lena says. Her voice is cracked. "I'm looking for my friend."

"No one has come in or out today."

The roar that had come from Hedy's mouth. The rage in her

eyes at Lena's appearance in the cave. And the beast—the lion on top of her.

Was she trapped? Angry? Lost?

"I have to find her."

"Madam, I assure you she isn't here."

Lena sidesteps the woman and heads for the door.

"Please wait," the concierge says. She reaches for Lena's arm, then recoils at the blood staining the robe. "Let me be of some assistance. First medical."

"I can't wait," Lena says.

"Please." The woman picks up the phone. "I need some assistance in the lobby," she says. Her tone urgent and cryptic.

And then Drew rushing from his villa, out of breath when he reaches the lobby.

"Mom."

"Where's Hedy?" Lena says.

"I'm sure she's around," Drew says.

Lena adjusts her robe and tightens the belt.

"She's not in her room, so where is she?"

"You're bleeding," Drew says.

"Where is she?"

"You need to get dressed. You need to get that cut looked at."

"I need to find Hedy."

"She's not here. She's probably sleeping it off on the beach."

Lena heads for the door again. This time Drew restrains her with a firm grip on her wrist. "She's probably fine, Mom. She's partying or whatever."

"She's blind, Drew. Almost." But last night Hedy hadn't seemed blind. Last night in the cave she had been able to see Lena clear as anything.

"She'll be fine. I'm sure she's stayed out all night before." He takes a step back—a deep breath. "Mom, please."

"I need to find my friend."

But the fury in Hedy's eyes. The roar.

"Listen, Mom. I was thinking of taking Jordan out for lunch. A change of scene. Come with us. Hedy will be back by the time we're done. And if not, we'll go look for her."

A deep breath and another.

She feels the pain in her arm for the first time. Feels the dirt on her skin.

"Mom."

Drew's voice—calm, reasonable.

The last time Hedy and Lena had been wild and free together Lena had paired off with Stavros. She'd endured Hedy's chilled anger. Her sidelong looks. Her snide comments. And now Hedy was the one who got lucky, as they used to say. The one who'd chosen a man over Lena. So maybe let her stew in it for a moment.

Lena showers and bandages the wound on her forearm. Her body is scraped all over. She chooses a long caftan that chafes her shredded skin. Her feet feel cramped in her delicate leather sandals. She looks at herself in the mirror. Gone is the wild beauty, the strange golden glow she had given off earlier. She looks diminished. Reduced. She has receded.

Lena tames her hair.

She puts on makeup—masking the natural glow left behind by the morning sun. She dabs her wrists with the bespoke perfume the hotel curated just for her.

They ride down the hill from the Agape in the same SUV that

had brought them from the airport. The windows are dark. The sky muted.

Lena cranes her neck as they pass the beach. A quick glimpse of the huddle of tents. And then the Agape property is behind them.

Jordan hasn't said a word since they got in the car. There's a tension in the way her hands knead the hem of her linen shift.

"Are you feeling okay?" Lena asks.

"She's fine," Drew says.

"Jordan?" Lena has never known Jordan not to speak for herself. And while Lena will admit that she doesn't have much in the way of maternal warmth for her daughter-in-law, she admires Jordan. Fears her a little too.

Jordan has always looked at Lena as if she can see right through her. See the demise and compromise that make up Lena's life. If Jordan didn't speak to her often, Lena didn't mind. Her cool regard was loud enough.

But Jordan's silence today is different. It's not frigid or judgmental. It's not standoffish.

"I'm fine," Jordan says. Her voice distant.

"Pregnancy is taxing," Drew says.

Lena tilts her head against the polarized window. "Is that so."

They take a coastal road around the island. Cheap resorts. Tourist towns. A glimpse of the sea now and then. Boat rentals.

The road narrows. The SUV lurches over uneven ground and they climb up a hill. A groan from Jordan.

"Would you like some fresh air?" Lena asks.

"We're almost there," Drew explains.

They park near a restaurant on a bluff overlooking the water. Drew helps Jordan from the car. A host leads them to a table outdoors where they can smell the sea and notes of wild basil and heather.

"It would be nice to go for a swim," Jordan says.

"Absolutely," Drew booms, slapping the table as if he's been told a terrific joke. "I'll call ahead and have them bring drinks to our pool and make sure the sunshades are in the right place."

"I'd prefer to swim in the ocean," Jordan says. She gestures toward the sea.

"Well," Drew says. "Soon."

"Drew, all that water. We are on an island. There's got to be some beach—" Jordan says.

"Until the situation on our beach is cleared up, it's going to have to be the pool."

"Clearly there are other beaches," Jordan says. The same tone she uses on Lena from time to time.

Lena sips her wine. "Exactly, Drew. You don't have to police everything. You don't have to decide for everyone."

"And I should let you make decisions?" Drew says. "You slept naked on a fucking beach, Mom."

"Drew," Jordan says. "We're on vacation. And I'd like to go to the beach, not the pool."

"Don't complicate things, please." Drew, firm and final. The conversation ends with the arrival of the waiter.

Drew orders for the table. A bad habit he picked up from his father. Meant to be charming and debonair but really selfish and showy. The waiter takes it all in, the dishes and the details of in what order Drew wants them to arrive. The small modifications. "And a half carafe of wine should do it."

"A full carafe," Jordan says.

A look from Drew. "That's not necessary."

"I'd like to have a glass today." A nod at the waiter. "A full carafe will be perfect." Her tone authoritative. A woman who gets what she wants. "Thank you," she says, dismissing him.

"It's not going to kill her," Lena says to Drew.

"You're one to talk," he replies, glowering at the turquoise water. "You're a shining example of moderation and safety."

"Did you actually sleep on the beach?" Jordan asks.

"I'm afraid I did," Lena says.

She waits for the shudder, the judgmental dismissal she's often received from Jordan.

"Was she there? The woman who came to the hotel?"

"Yes, of course," Lena says.

"And did she say anything?" Jordan asks.

Drew reaches for Jordan's hand. "Like my mother is in any position to remember what anyone said last night."

"About what?" Lena asks.

Jordan pulls away from Drew's grip. "About me."

Lena laughs. "I don't think so. Why would she say something about you?"

Drew's free hand—a fist on the table. "I'm not going to sit here and listen to another word about that lunatic and her freeloading gypsies. Today or tomorrow they will be gone and that is the end of it. Do you two understand? No more discussion."

Jordan's eyes never leave Drew's as the waiter fills her glass and she takes a long, generous sip. "Is Hedy still with them?" she asks Lena.

Lena shivers despite the warmth. Hedy, alone on the beach. But perhaps not really alone. "I assume," she says. "I don't know."

BEFORE

went with them to Greece. I told myself I was just biding time until Phaex Fest on Corfu. I had stocked up and I had more coming. I was ready. For one wild weekend I would be the ruler of the Ionian Sea.

But first, BaXXus wanted us to go to Naxos.

BaXXus told us that he was twice-born, once from his mother, then again through his father. Whatever that meant.

He said that he was being reborn for a third time through us—or them—his women. That they gave him life and strength and he was nothing without them.

I've been around this scene—and others—long enough to have heard all sorts of tripped-out nonsense. Everyone is always being reborn into knowledge, into a new body, a new mind, a new gender, a new awareness, a new, new, new whatever. Everyone always making everything into a bigger deal than it needs to be—ascribing beauty and freedom to a fucking rave.

You are the ones who bring me to life.

The women swarmed him, pawed him, opened their mouths to lick his skin.

"I thought it was the other way around," I said.

He took us to an ancient shrine—the ruin of a temple in the village of Yria.

His golden eyes on mine. *Do you still not believe who I am?*

I have seen people resurrected from near-fatal overdoses. I've seen people survive falls from fourth-story windows, from the sides of yachts, from the scaffolding over a main stage. I have witnessed the beautiful and terrifying transformation of friends and strangers—skin peeled back, the true monster revealed.

So maybe if you do what I do, it's helpful to imagine that there's something larger than the banal desire to get off your head. Maybe there is a lord of the dance. A hand that reaches out and guides us.

It wouldn't be the wildest thing I'd considered—encountered—if this man were divine.

In the temple, the women went wild. They wrapped themselves around the crumbling columns and writhed on the ground like serpents.

"What are you doing to them?" I asked. "What are they taking?"

They are becoming part of me.

"Is that why they glow?"

They are glowing. They are stronger. It is not an illusion. For a moment, they are semidivine.

He held out his hand. I knew better than to take it.

His skin, his sweat, his aura was the drug.

We walked down from the temple, through olive groves and hills covered with heather. I could smell each fragrance as a separate element. I could taste the gray-green olives without picking them.

We walked through a terraced vineyard where the air had the bouquet of wine.

Behind us I could hear the women following. But BaXXus somehow kept them at a distance.

They were keening. Howling. They were hungry in their mad pursuit.

"You should let them go," I said.

Is that what you would do?

"They're your slaves."

Followers.

"You're controlling them."

You do the same.

"I don't take prisoners."

That is a matter of opinion.

"You are using them."

They are using me. Without my strength they will be weak.

"And without them would you be weak also?"

My drug is others' belief. Without it I fade away.

I understood. He makes them strong so they make him strong— a snake in its own endless circle. Except that their power is fleeting, fades when his drug wears off. While his—it grows and grows.

We kept walking. We passed a stream. I stooped to drink and the water tasted like wine. I sensed animals all around us, following our progress but keeping their distance.

"I don't take prisoners," I repeated.

Do you despise women so much that you think they can't make their own decisions?

"It's a cult," I said.

There are worse things. Imagine never seeing into the ecstatic heart of the world. Imagine never knowing colors for what they truly are or tasting the actual fruit of the vine. I give that to them. I am giving it to you.

The hillside was vibrating—the colors glowing with the heightened exaggeration of a balanced hallucination. The air was sweet and rich—tinged with an exotic honeyed flavor.

What you see now—what you sense—imagine never experiencing these things. Those things.

A wave of his arm.

Imagine never seeing the secret world of this hillside. Imagine forever seeing the world through a dirty lens. Through dark glasses, your ears muffled and cotton in your mouth. With me, you will never be so blind.

"I've seen the world this way," I said. "I've made it happen on my own." It was true. There were nights when I was able to name every snowflake and tell my future in the dust motes of a strobe light.

But your way will destroy you in the end.

There was truth in his words. At my age, each pill drives the next high farther out of reach. And I feared that one day those highs would be gone altogether and all I would have left would be the people who need what I sell. A magician cut off from her magic.

"And your way won't?"

He didn't answer.

We had come to the bottom of the hillside. I could see small waves breaking on the sand. The women had caught up to us, whatever barrier he had put in place removed. They encircled him, pushing me out.

He pointed to the beach. *That is my sacred home. I will make it ours.*

_____

didn't stay with them. There was a boutique hotel above the beach but it was still under construction. A collection of villas each with its own pool.

checked into a tourist trap in the old town. The nightlife scene was pretty tame—the same old, same old chillwave soundtrack. None of the up-tempo stuff you see on the other islands—booming nightclubs with five-star sound systems and A-list DJs.

I planned to set up shop, certain I'd be the only game in town. Vacationers are fish in a barrel—everyone wanting to heighten their getaway, everyone wanting to see through into "the ecstatic heart of the world," as BaXXus called it. And I would be their portal.

Except there was competition.

The women.

His women.

They began to arrive in the old town. They looked disheveled and deranged to me but now carried more of his golden glow. Had it transferred? Had it rubbed off? Were they transforming?

They were magnetic.

They trailed music and some strange earthy funk that was repellent and intoxicating. They wound their way through the upscale bars and small clubs. They danced to music only they could hear. They left golden contrails in the air and soon vacationing women started to follow in their wake.

These vacationers—I recognized the type. Reformed party girls trapped in respectable costumes. Women just like you. Women who once cut loose in clubs and bars and on the sand, now hidden away in luxe caftans, counting calories and drinks, measuring and moderating—their joy gone. Until BaXXus's women came for them. And then they shed their second skins and stepped back out into the night.

I kept watch.

Night after night, I saw the vacationers depart, chasing BaXXus's women. I saw them return the next morning enveloped in some of BaXXus's aura—their eyes gold-glittered, the scent of wine and forest cloaking them.

I noticed that some didn't come back. But the ones who did, they didn't want what I had.

I sat at the bar at Oceanus. Two women took the stools next to me. They were gushing, mad-high, a flood of overblown emotions.

He touched me.

He spoke to me.

He told me we needed to come back. That I needed to come back. That he needed me.

I knew of course.

It's weird right, but the taste of his sweat. You know what I mean.

The bartender came over. "Drinks, ladies?"

They held up their hands in refusal.

"Taking it easy for once?" he asked.

"Our bodies are temples."

The bartender met my eye. "That's not the way it looked earlier this week." He refilled my wine. "This island does strange things to people."

I followed the women outside. I don't push. I let them come. But I needed to see. "Big night, ladies?" I asked. "Where's the party?"

They took my hand and spun me in circles. "Come with us. You have to come. You need to meet the golden god."

"A god?" I asked. "This I have to see." I reached into my pocket. "Why don't you take a few of these. On the house. Enhance the experience."

The women recoiled from me. "God no," one of them barked. "We can't bring that stuff near him. We can't touch him if we are . . . high."

"Why not?" I asked. "What happens?"

"Those drugs are poison."

I laughed. "To who?"

"We want him strong. We make him strong. That's what he told us. We are all he needs."

They looked at the pills in my hand as if they were something dead and fetid.

"Pick your poison," I said. I headed back to the bar and popped a pill.

I waited for the come-up.

I waited to see the distorted edges of solid objects.

I waited for the first tiptoe on my flesh, the fingers to crawl up my arms and turn up my heartbeat.

I waited for the first neural flutter.

It never came. Nothing. Not a twinge or a twitch. Not the slightest quickening. The end had come. I'd been at this too long. I'd run dry.

My mind remained clear and in that clarity I formed a plan to return the women to me.

DREW

Collective mania. Mass hysteria. It doesn't take a sociologist or psychologist to figure out what's happening. You see it in all sectors. Online social media–driven fads for dangerous practices—swallowing cinnamon, eating dishwasher pods, cooking NyQuil-basted chicken. Anti-vaxxers. Bioterrorist alarmists. And now, post-COVID, everyone an epidemiologist. People mired in their own personal pandemics. Inventing necessary precautions. Self-diagnosing.

His mother, clearly overwhelmed by grief. Jordan, destabilized by hormones. And Hedy—well, Hedy is just fucking insane. A canary in the coal mine for this sort of shit.

Look how close he himself had come to falling under the same spell. How he had almost been tricked into seeing his mother as some sort of powerful creature when she had returned from the beach.

Nonsense and lies. Stories we tell ourselves to excuse our own stupidity.

You can't argue with crazy. You can only restore order.

So let Jordan have this one glass of wine. Don't comment.

Ignore the scratches and scrapes on his mother's flesh. (Seriously, what the fuck.) Ignore the bandaged wound on her arm. Addressing these things only gives them power and meaning. Makes them real as opposed to the dregs of some deranged fantasy.

So just wait. The minute those women are cleared from his beach this insanity will recede like a bad dream. The hotel will open. The social media accounts will be flooded with the right sort of images posted by the right sort of guests. Then he and Jordan will return to the stability of their life in New York.

He indulges them during lunch. He orders more food. Confident that this afternoon is in hand. They need to try these island specialties. Local catch too. A tray of desserts. Perhaps another. Please bring out the chef so we can thank him. Generous. Thoughtful. Instructive. A guide and a guardian. This is Drew's show, after all.

Don't forget that.

In the car he calls the hotel to make sure special attention will be paid to setting up the pool area for Jordan that afternoon. Perhaps the Reiki or chakra balancing. For Lena too. Keep them close. Keep them pampered. Make them forget.

He pretends not to notice his mother craning her neck for a better view of the beach encampment as they turn up the hill to the hotel.

He pretends not to notice Jordan's unusual silence in the car.

He keeps talking. Filling the air.

Distracting them. Putting on a show.

Talking so much and so loudly that he doesn't notice the woman from the beach is standing in the Agape's driveway. He doesn't have enough time to keep Jordan and Lena out of her reach as they exit the car.

"Luz!" His mother greeting her like an old friend.

Drew will not speak to this woman. There is nothing to say.

He takes Jordan by the arm. "Come on."

"You went into the cave," Luz says to Lena. "What did you see?"

Drew looks at his mother. "Cave?"

"What did you see?"

"Where is Hedy?" Lena asks.

"She's staying with us now."

"Fantastic. That's just great," Drew says. "I give her a two-thousand-dollar-a-night suite and she wants to go camping."

"Don't you want to see her?" Luz asks Lena.

"No, she doesn't," Drew says. "And after tomorrow, none of us will be seeing any of you."

Luz steps in front of him. Look at her. Giant and wild. A big, hot arrogant mess. Imagine falling under the spell of this dirty, unhinged creature.

But she's not exactly dirty. Not in the way Drew would expect. None of the grit and sand that were streaked across his mother's body this morning. There's something radiant about her. Commanding.

Drew looks away. He doesn't want to acknowledge anything about this woman except for the fact that she's a lunatic.

"Do not try and move us," she says.

He stares at a spot over her shoulder, unwilling to meet her gaze. "Or you'll do me like you did my father."

"Your father, like you, picked a battle he couldn't win. But we did nothing to him that he didn't do to himself. If he was weak, he shouldn't have come to us. I'd say the same to you."

"Are you threatening me?"

"No," Luz says. He can feel her eyes boring into him. He can feel her compelling him to meet her gaze. He will not look. "I'm just telling you what will happen."

There are boats in the water. A large yacht perhaps carrying the sort of guests who will soon fill the Agape. The air is sweet with the precise basil smell Drew had bottled and turned into room fragrances for guests to purchase and take home. The driveway's plantings are perfect—a meticulous design that's meant to evoke the casual growth on the surrounding hillsides. The music coming from the concealed speakers is the perfect chillwave cover of eighties pop songs. In three days, the hotel will open, cementing Drew's ascent to his father's throne. His first solo success.

But why isn't Jordan heading into the hotel? And why the fuck is his mother hanging on this woman's words as if they weren't being spoken by a crazy person?

Luz reaches for Jordan's arm. Drew jerks her away. A gasp from Jordan, like he's the one who hurt her.

"Tell me," Luz says. "Are you still feeling sick?"

"She's fine," Drew says.

"Tell me if your stomach still hurts. Tell me if that monster is making you sick. Tell me if that monster is trying to get out."

"Enough." He doesn't care how much force he has to exert. He grabs Jordan's wrist, twisting the skin, making it burn. But he has no choice. He has to get her away from this woman. He pulls Jordan into the hotel. He leaves his mother behind. She's a lost cause anyway.

They did a good job on the pool setup. Hard to add luxury to luxury, but it's been done. The playlist curated. A bartender providing nonalcoholic craft cocktails inspired by the island. The facialist already in place.

"Relax," Drew says to Jordan.

He watches the bartender fix her a drink made from lemon and basil and some other herbs. He watches her sit in the chair brought by the aesthetician.

He checks his watch.

Just over twenty-four hours and those women will be gone. But for now Drew will try to enjoy what he has built—the fine details, the extravagant touches. He will get a massage with oil made from local olives. He will control the temperature of the pools, and when the sun begins to set, he will fiddle with the subaquatic lighting to create the perfect lightscape.

After a while Jordan sends the bartender and the aesthetician away. He lets her. He understands that she wants to be alone. In a few hours he will find his mother and see if Hedy is back. Then there will be dinner in his suite. Tomorrow, he will get back to the business of the hotel.

They have nearly dressed for dinner when Drew opens the door to his suite to find Officer Gabris, his eyes dark and his brow lowered.

The policeman rubs his hands together and exhales loudly.

"What?" Drew says. "What now?"

"Mr. Baros. I'm sorry but we are going to have to delay our operation."

"Operation? Has this turned into a military-grade procedure? All I'm asking is for you to move twenty women off my beach."

"It appears that it's not your beach. There is some validity to the cultural importance of the cave."

"It's a fucking cave and this is a luxury hotel. Don't you see how twisted that is? I have value. That doesn't."

"We are still assessing the situation."

Drew pulls back into the suite. "Jordan, call my mother. Tell her to get over here right now."

The officer is still talking. "These things can take time and they must be handled carefully."

Human rights. Governmental cooperation. UNESCO. It goes in one ear and out the other.

Drew's anger is molten. White-hot rage floods every goddamn inch of his body. He wants to choke this man right here and now.

"Surely it would be better for everyone if these wild women were not raising hell on that beach regardless of whether it is mine or not?"

"There are considerations."

"Honestly, fuck these considerations."

Here's his goddamn mess of a mother at last. Look at the state of her. That fucking caftan hiding fucking nothing. "Mom." To think that morning he'd thought of her as anything more than a saggy fifty-four-year-old ex-ballerina.

Her eyes widen at his tone, but fuck that too.

"Mom. Tell me. You went in that cave."

No response. What the fuck is wrong with her? "The cave. On the beach."

"I looked inside."

"And what did you see?"

What is that look on Lena's face?

"I'm not sure."

"You're not sure what you saw?"

"I mean—I saw a lion."

"A lion?"

"A golden lion."

"Honestly, Mom. What the fuck?"

"You asked."

"But no ruins? No temple. Nothing of cultural importance. Just a fucking lion?"

"That's what I saw."

Drew turns from his mother to Officer Gabris. "You see what I'm dealing with? You see what those creatures are doing to my mother? A lion? There was no fucking lion."

"That's what I saw," Lena insists.

When did she go full lunatic on him? Was it after Dad died? Because Dad died? Was it Hedy's fault? Or those nutjobs on the beach?

"You see," he says to Officer Gabris. "Those women tricked my mother into seeing a lion. They made her hallucinate. And who knows what they did to my father."

"Drew—your father died of a heart attack," Lena says.

A look at the officer. That man's fucking self-satisfied smile. Like Drew's the problem, not those fuckers on the beach.

"This is nonsense," Drew says. He bangs his fist on the doorframe. "Total utter fucking nonsense. You know what my mother got up to down there. You saw how high those women were. This isn't safe."

"But it isn't illegal," Officer Gabris says. "We'll see what we can do. But for now, we have to leave the encampment alone."

"Is that so?" Drew says. He's losing it, he knows. If he's not careful he's going to lower his worth in the eyes of this fucking local policeman. But this is one fucking outrageous fuckfest of a problem. "Well, then maybe it's better if I handle it my own way."

"Sir, I strongly discourage you from doing that."

"Don't you fucking tell me what to do."

JORDAN

She's certain. The woman gave it a name—monster—and then Jordan knew. The very thing she feared created out of her own fear.

In classrooms, in job interviews, in boardrooms, she'd always spoken up. Always stated her purpose, her intention. Taken a stand.

She wanted children. But not now. Not so soon. Not on Drew's timeline or his terms. She thought the choice would be hers.

She thought she could live with his decision.

Instead, she is incubating a creature born from her weakness—one that will devour her.

Weak like her mother. Weak like Lena. Why now? Why this failure when she knew the outcome? All that education, self-control, and acquired power and she hadn't progressed at all.

No better than the countless stay-at-home mothers, the unhappy, hapless housewives that she disdained.

Inside her, a creature conceived from her hesitation. Fed by her anxiety. Nurtured by her fear. Growing stronger with each of Jordan's negative thoughts.

The thing inside her is swelling. It hasn't let her sleep in two days. She can feel it. Twisting and clawing.

She feels it like a sickness, a cancer.

She feels its talons digging in.

It knows.

It will spite her.

She hates it and it hates her—a literal snake eating its own tail until it turns its fangs on her.

And now, its teeth piercing her organs.

Is it determined to get out or does it want to stay inside and grow?

Like a parasite. An invasive species.

But she had no choice. It was there before she knew it. Drew had put it in her and she had let it stay. A monster of her own making. Her fault for creating it. Carrying it.

Her own hubris for keeping it.

For imagining it is anything other than what it is.

If only she had said no.

No one ever asks.

They just assume.

Even when you look as if you are in control, it's a false front.

Always playing catch-up in the business world. Then regressing, backsliding into roles written before time was time.

She'd traded one costume for another. The inoffensive office neutrals for the false glow of motherhood. She would do it right, prove her mother wrong. Despite her hesitation, she would triumph as she always did. So what, she wasn't ready. She would be.

But it didn't work like that.

The hesitation was an infection. Then a sickness. Then a plague. She couldn't let it show. Wouldn't.

Until that woman saw.

And then it was too late to keep on pretending.

Jordan can feel the creature. It's devouring her. It's consuming her and eating her alive as it grows.

It's feeding on her. And she is allowing it to do so, because that's what mothers do. She's protecting it.

She can feel it snaking through her body. Wrapping its tentacles around her organs. It's gripping her tight. It's strangling her.

Not even fully grown and it's already a killer.

We bear the monsters that kill us.

Each one of us responsible for bringing horror into the world.

Every one of us guilty. Genocide. Chemical warfare. Environmental destruction on all of our consciences.

We bear the agents of our own destruction.

Sometimes we aren't given a choice.

But sometimes we are.

DREW

Only fools wait. Only fools allow things to happen to them. Omegas. B-types. Team players, not leaders. Eternal benchwarmers.

Stavros's empire, from the flick of a match. But that's a story they don't tell in the boardroom. He knew, of course. He knew it all, knew how his father had burned those people out of their slum. And so what? Opportunity costs.

Ask, answer, act—the foundational principles of any leader. What's the problem? What's the solution? When is it time to take action?

The answer is obvious. Now.

Drew could give a TED Talk on this shit.

Who will make the change, if not me? What would another person do in my place?

Jordan is groaning in her sleep. Another reason he must act. Before this trip, she'd been a tranquil sleeper. Now it looks as if she's drowning.

He slips out of bed. He feels Jordan grasping for his hand, as if she wants him to save her.

"I'll be right back."

The twenty-four-hour concierge is in place. And thank god, should Lena try anything stupid. A quick nod. He's a business owner inspecting his property. Doing his job. Nothing more.

The lights in the driveway are on their overnight setting—a warm glow that illuminates the facades of the Agape Villas like the Parthenon while also conveying a sense of vigilance and security.

He snakes down the driveway, crosses the road to the first stretch of the dune grasses at the top of the beach.

Drew reaches into his pocket for a lighter.

His father's son after all.

The dried grass catches quickly.

Another spot and another—the vegetation up in flames.

In the moon's glimmer, Drew can see the tents and tarps.

He checks once to make sure they are in the fire's path. Then he heads back to his hotel.

JORDAN

Drew is gone. Swallowed into the night.

The monster inside is kicking.

It feels fully grown. It feels impossible to contain it any longer.

She wants to birth it, to see the horror of her creation. And then she will destroy it.

Her fear baby. The child of her weakness.

She feels it pressing against her abdomen. Punching her.

She feels it in her throat. She will speak with its voice.

The door to the suite is open. The echo of Drew's footfalls heading away.

The monster kicks and twists.

It coos its hate-song inside her head.

It growls.

It will rip her stomach apart if she doesn't move. If she doesn't take action. If she doesn't release it, it will kill her.

Down the hall after Drew as if she can outrun the creature that is inside her.

He's out the door.

Jordan hangs back. Then follows.

The night is a relief. It calms the tumult in her body. She drinks the air greedily.

Drew is at the base of the driveway. He is crossing the road.

Jordan watches. Then she loses him in the night.

She sees him again—a silhouette against a fire rising from the dunes.

She sees the monster that Lena bore.

The selfish architect of the flames that are surging from the beach.

And then she runs.

LENA

The light outside has shifted. It glows. Not with the sun. With something else.

Lena gets out of bed.

She has kept the doors to the patio open hoping—for what? A sound or a summons from the beach. Hedy's laughter carried by the wind.

Instead, she hears crackling. And a shout.

Lena rushes to the patio.

More cries.

Flames frame the beach parallel to the road.

The night is still. No breeze. The voices from the camp carry. Louder and louder as the flames rise.

Back inside, through the hotel, through the lobby, and out onto the driveway.

The hotel is coming to life.

The flames higher now. Any breeze and they will sweep across the beach, devouring the encampment.

There's Drew coming up the driveway not calling for help or rushing for water. "Drew!" Lena grabs her son's arm.

"Let it burn," he says. "The outcome is the same either way."

The women on the beach are shouting, their cries shredding the night.

"Hedy is down there."

"Not for long," Drew says. "See, there's a favor I've done you. Got your friend to come home."

"You could kill someone."

"That shouldn't matter to you."

"Drew!"

"You're living on blood wealth, Mom. Don't lie to yourself."

A different fire—two stories of an SRO destroyed as collateral.

"It will just wake them up. Get them moving."

The air is starting to smell of burning grass and the sweet scent of heather and other herbs going up in smoke. There is movement on the beach. The women are coming from their tents.

"You see," Drew says. "It's working."

"Help them." Lena feels her skin tighten around her bones. She feels her flesh harden—her exoskeleton clamp down over the self she'd released on the beach last night.

When the fire reaches the tents, it will take that self away. It will consume and destroy the Lena that she'd only just set free.

Lena falls to her knees with a cry.

"Don't be so dramatic, Mom," Drew says.

The flames are rising, obscuring the edge of the beach.

And then the fire turns. Reverses course. All at once, like an army being called to retreat. Instead of eating up the beach until it reaches the tents, it leaps the road. It skims across the asphalt like mercury and starts to climb the hill to the Agape.

The fire is hungry. Starved. It wastes no time with the plantings as it runs uphill.

The hotel is a cacophony of cries.

A fire truck wails in the distance.

Drew races to the entrance. Lena behind him, chased by the fire. From the communal dining area they watch the flames destroy the driveway.

Drew is rage and fury. Screaming at the firemen. Screaming at everyone to bring water. Screaming and screaming and screaming.

The entire hill is blanketed in flames, as if the fire knew exactly where it wanted to go. As if it had a target, and an end point. As if it weren't wild and uncontrolled but a driven, determined entity.

And then the fire is vanquished at the doorway to the Agape. Like it didn't intend to come any closer, it gives way to the hoses and buckets. But still, the white walls are smudged with soot. The air smells charred. The plantings reduced to ash.

"How—how," Drew stammers. Then his eyes grow cold and still. "She turned it back. That witch from the beach. She turned it. She made it come this way."

He pushes past the last fireman, back out to the driveway.

The smoke is lifting. Lena can see the beach. She can see the women from the camp standing in a line on their side of the road. If Hedy is there, Lena cannot pick her out of the crowd.

Behind them, the sun begins to rise. The ocean turns purple, then orange, then red.

Drew makes his way to the end of the driveway.

One woman breaks from the crowd and stands in the middle of the road.

It's not someone Lena recognizes from the beach. It's not Hedy. It's Jordan.

She wears a white silk camisole and pajama shorts.

From the waist down, her clothes are smeared with blood.

Blood streams down her legs and puddles on the road.

She runs her hands down her legs, then smears the blood on her face.

And she smiles.

The women move from the beach. They encircle Jordan. Then she is gone.

DREW

He rushes across the road. He doesn't see the car that swerves to miss him. Burning rubber in addition to the char in the air.

The women are disappearing into the dunes.

They have Jordan.

"Stop."

The burned grass crackles under his feet. He trips, dives face-first, the soot and ash filling his nose.

And then Luz is in front of him. She reaches for his hand and pulls him to his feet.

"Go," she says. She points at the Agape.

"Give me back Jordan."

"She's not yours."

"What have you done to her?"

"Us? We haven't done anything."

All that blood. All that blood. "She's bleeding."

"Not anymore."

"She's going to die."

"Not anymore."

"What happened to the baby?"

"She didn't want the baby."

Drew balls his hands into fists.

"She's safe with us."

"No. You'll kill her." The dirt. The sand. That blood. "Give her back!"

"She's not mine to give."

Drew cups his hands around his mouth. "Jordan!"

"We are taking care of her. Then we will let her decide."

"There's no decision," Drew says. "There's no decision to be made. Jordan belongs with me."

"There's always a decision. You can decide whether to spark a flame and start a fire. A fire can decide which way it wants to burn. You can decide to keep or lose the monster someone has put inside you."

He reaches for Luz's neck. She steps back. "There's no fucking monster. That's a lie you told her."

"How can you be so sure?" Her green snake eyes leach poison in the rising sun. "If you want to see Jordan, you know where to find her."

BEFORE

was armed.

In my fist, fifty of my best pills. The ones I upsell to the richest clients telling them just one and they'll see god, and two—they'll be god. In my backpack I had other supplies.

I found the women in a cave in the side of a small cliff at the edge of the beach.

I tracked them by the golden light that was emanating from the cave's mouth.

They were sitting around BaXXus, who reclined shirtless on the ground, his eyes closed, his skin glowing. Amber beads of sweat dripped down his muscled chest.

So this was BaXXus's holy site—this dank cave his sacred domain where they carried out his rites.

I've seen weirder. I've been in worse.

I've seen the grimiest warehouse turned into an astral plane, an underwater wonderland, a through-the-looking-glass world. I know that transcendence happens in the most unlikely places.

Are you wondering how I dared carry out my plan? How I believed I could trap a god?

Remember, I've held entire fields of people captive over three-day weekends.

I've held you captive.

I've held entire four-story mega-clubs under my thumb.

I've done what you think is impossible. So why not do this?

I bet big on his hubris.

I bet that he imagined I'd come to heel.

That I was his.

Because that is divine weakness—imagining that you are enough and that when you reveal yourself to us—when we finally see you—we will always love you.

BaXXus parted the women so I could step through. He didn't see me fill my mouth with the pills.

His women scurried away, obedient, but their faces were clouded with anger.

I knelt at his side.

He turned his cheek, an invitation for me to drink from his skin. But I pointed at his mouth. The source.

He opened his mouth.

I pressed mine to his and released the pills. He gagged with surprise. He sputtered. Some went flying, others he swallowed.

And he was mine.

His golden eyes closed. He writhed and convulsed. The women shrieked. I held them off and then, pulling chains from my bag, I bound him.

I cleared the women out of the cave. But they lingered at the mouth, their eyes on my prisoner. He was asleep or unconscious or in whatever state gods go to when they are not with us.

The women howled.

"You're free to leave," I told them.

But they didn't want to.

I saw the look in their eyes. *The look.* The one I saw on my own face reflected in the god's golden irises back in Portugal. The look I love and despise.

By morning, some of the women's sheen had come off. They were less glorious. Less magnificent. More human. Their funky scent had become a stink.

I couldn't bear to look at them.

"Go," I hollered.

They didn't go. They came closer. Their hunger was growing. And I had what they needed.

If skin and sweat are potent, surely blood must be more so.

And since gods cannot die, only weaken, I took a chance.

I slit him along his ribs and filled two bottles with his golden blood.

By the time I returned from passing the bottles to the women, the cuts had healed.

I squatted at the god's side. I didn't know how long I could hold him—can hold him. The women's belief—their need—would keep him alive. But I would be the conduit, the one pulling the strings. To get to him, they would have to go through me.

That night they gathered around me. I let them drink. They clung to me.

"Go," I shouted. "Dance."

And they danced.

"Stop."

They stopped.

"Dance."

They began again.

They danced all night at my command and into the next day and the next week.

They danced until one evening a well-dressed gentleman appeared.

He wanted to see inside the cave.

I told him he could if only he would dance.

Then I danced him down like I'd seen BaXXus do to the woman at Dreamwerks nearly a year ago. I danced him until he tore up the sand. I danced him while my women clapped and cheered. I danced him and danced him and then I watched him stagger away, his hand to his heart.

And I never saw him again.

You wonder why I don't let them go.

There was a moment when I planned to.

But they were mine before they were his.

I wanted to keep them close. I wanted to swell their ranks. I wanted to open their minds and punish them for their stupidity for allowing themselves to be captive.

I wanted to punish them, and you, for seeing me as a dirty peddler of dirty things—someone to discard and disdain in the daylight hours.

I will make them bring you to me.

I will make you dance and I will hold you until you are mine and then I may destroy you or keep you.

His power is mine now. I will make you strong. I will make you see. I will make you know the world as you have never known it, never seen it.

It is what I've always done.

And you won't be able to resist me.

LENA

It's evening. The fire trucks are long gone. A cleanup crew has finished raking the burned vegetation from the driveway and buffing the smoke damage from the Agape's facade.

Lena kept her distance from the activity. Kept her distance from Drew too—his face rage-red and grief-sallow. She thought it would be too much to confront him for what he had done and what was done to him.

But when he knocks, she lets him in. Drew is her son after all.

"She'll come back," Lena says.

"I don't want to talk about her."

The sun begins to set. The infinity pool's lights come on.

Drew closes the door to the patio. He pulls the curtains as if he can erase the outside world—the burned hillside, the beach, the rest of it.

He orders dinner that they don't eat.

He orders wine but it has no taste.

Lena sits on the couch and watches Drew pace like a caged animal. He checks the door to the patio, making sure it's locked. He checks the front door. Then he falls down next to her, his head in her lap.

A lonely, lost little boy in a big hotel. She strokes his hair, because that's what mothers do.

"What a fucking mess. Can I sleep here tonight?"

"Of course," Lena says.

Her fingers in his hair, combing, raking, trying to put everything back into place. A mother's job to make it right.

"I want to kill her. I want to kill all of them."

"Drew, shh."

"What kind of power does that woman have over you?"

"I don't know, sweetheart. I don't know if she has any at all."

"What does she do to you? What does she say?"

"Nothing special."

"What goes on down there?"

"You have to see for yourself."

How long has it been since she was alone with Drew like this? How long since he seemed to need her?

"If Jordan doesn't come back, I'll go get her for you," Lena says.

"Thank you, Mom."

How long has it been since he thanked her?

They sit in silence, watching the sky darken.

"I would love it if you did that. If you did that for me."

She feels Drew drifting off. His breath changing, deepening. His heart rate slowing.

"I can sleep here, right, Mom?"

"Of course, sweetheart."

And how long since she's called him anything but Drew?

Lena watches her son sleep. For years, she could still see the baby and the child in his face. But now that is gone. Just a man trying so hard to be his father.

She lets him remain there, head in her lap, until her legs grow numb. Then she slides out. She stands over him, watching him at peace for once. She goes to her bedroom and closes the door.

In her dream there is a demon at her breast—a creature that chews and scratches. With each greedy sip it grows until it is twice Lena's size. It grows until she is reduced to nothing, sucked dry. She is a shriveled mass, the demon looming over her, ready to trample her to dust.

She wakes with a gasp. The room is still and stuffy. She has tossed the sheets onto the floor. She has clawed her own breast, adding to the wounds from the pup she'd suckled, the bruise from when her heart was torn out, and the scratches from the fingernails of the women on the beach as they stripped her flesh.

Lena flings open her bedroom door. Drew is not on the couch. He is not in the other bedrooms.

"Andrew?"

The air in the suite is close and cloying. Lena coughs.

She tries to open the door to the patio. But it is locked. The bolt doesn't budge.

She needs fresh air.

She tries the front door.

It doesn't open.

She bangs and bangs and bangs.

She calls her son's name. But no one comes for her. She tries the phone but the line is dead.

The suite seems to be draining of air. Impossible, she knows.

Lena can't breathe. She can't breathe.

She's been put on lockdown. A security threat. A threat to herself and others.

She beats the door, bruising her wrists and hands. She screams herself hoarse.

No one. No one comes.

She whirls around the room looking for something, anything. She lifts a dining stool and drives it against the glass patio door over and over again until her arms ache: the glass cracks and then shatters.

An avalanche of air. She can breathe again.

Now that Lena is free, her panic subsided, she can rage at her imprisonment. Her son, whom she let sleep on her lap, had trapped her. He'd tricked her. An insidious plan from the moment he showed up at her door.

She cuts her foot on the broken glass. She rinses it in the pool, watching the blood disperse through the water.

She can hear music from the beach. Even before she broke the patio door, she knew that there was only one place for her to go.

The music calls to her. The women are singing her down the hill, through the dunes, across the sand.

There they are dancing with ecstatic abandon.

They are standing in a semicircle, hands reaching toward her, pulling her close.

There's Luz, glorious in her arrogant beauty.

Lena steps into their circle. She knows what comes next. She will dance and dance and dance and she will never stop dancing until she has shown Drew the full force of her strength. And she will never let anyone trap her again.

DREW

They are deranged creatures. They are wild witches. They are grotesque and feral animals. There is nothing beautiful, powerful, or magical here. Just hideous mayhem and dangerous behavior.

Drew watches the women from up in the dunes. He hears their nonsensical cries. Their tuneless song that sounds like screaming coyotes. There's Hedy, the whole deluded, disorderly mess of her, lunging around like a blind drunk. There's Luz off to the side, passing around bottles of wine. Keeping track. Keeping tabs. Her eyes on the whole scene—conducting.

They think that they are dancing but it's nothing more than violent, spastic lurching. As if they are being electrocuted. Nothing graceful about it.

Where is Jordan? Is she bleeding out in that cave? Is she letting strangers touch her—their dirty hands on her body. Is she drinking from their communal bottle of wine, their spit in her mouth?

Drew shudders as some of the women howl, their heads tilted

toward the sky. They strip off their clothes. Like the world needs to see their flesh.

They raise their arms to the sky, howling and howling, as if they are calling some sort of devil.

They form a half circle, their backs to the fire, their hands reaching toward someone or something up the beach. Summoning. Their voices growing louder and more insistent. Shrieking. Drew covers his ears.

Someone or something is coming down the beach. The women wail and wave their hands as if they are pulling on an invisible rope.

Then Drew watches as his mother enters the circle of firelight.

LENA

Luz steps from the circle, beautiful in her arrogance.

"Where is Hedy? Jordan?"

"Come," Luz says, "let me show you."

They cross the sand. A golden glow leaks from the cave's mouth. Lena hesitates. Had she really seen a lion? Is that possible?

"There's nothing to be afraid of," Luz says.

Inside there is no lion, only a man. But he's more than a man. Superhuman, naked, his skin giving off a golden luminescence. He's larger than any man Lena has seen before—like a statue from antiquity. Long curls of reddish hair tumble down his shoulders.

He's naked and chained. A manacle on either wrist.

Two slits beneath his ribs leak golden blood.

And yet—he doesn't look diminished. He looks divine.

But still. "Who is that?"

"He's ours." Hedy rises from the cave floor.

"Ours?"

Hedy swipes a finger beneath one of the wounds and puts it to her lips. "Try."

Jordan emerges from the back of the cave, the top half of her clothes stained with the man's golden blood, the bottom with her own red blood. Her mouth is ringed in gold. Jordan licks the man's wounds.

How had Lena never noticed the beauty underneath Jordan's austere facade. "Jordan, your baby."

"It wasn't a baby."

"You need a doctor."

"She has everything she needs," Luz says. "We have taken care of her."

Luz shoos Hedy from the chained man, then holds a wine bottle to his rib cage and lets it fill, then offers it to Lena. "Perhaps you would prefer it this way."

Lena stares at Jordan, taking in the carnage. She should be sickened. She should be horrified. She should be concerned.

Instead, she's envious. How had Jordan set herself free from the same trap that had been set for Lena? How had she done the unthinkable?

She glances at the bottle. Is that what it took? Is that where she got the strength?

There's Hedy, desperate to lick the man's wounds, her eyes bright and focused.

"Drink," Luz says. "Take back what is yours."

The prison of her suite at the Agape. The prison in the Park Avenue penthouse. The ornate Pacific Heights Victorian.

"I love you," Hedy says. "I love you and I miss you and I've missed you for years because you disappeared." She rises and moves to Lena. She takes her in her arms and kisses her on the mouth. "I want you back."

Lena reaches for the bottle and she drinks.

It doesn't take long. The light in the cave grows brighter. The horror of the scene recedes. She feels the first ecstatic current inside her.

Lena grabs Jordan's hand.

She is beautiful and strong. How had Lena never noticed that before.

She pulls Jordan from the cave, pulls her free of Drew's shadow, and leads her to the dance.

DREW

He sees them—his mother and Jordan, hand in hand emerging from the cave. He watches his mother lead his wife toward the leaping flames.

In the firelight he can see that Jordan is smeared with blood from the waist down. Something gold drips from her mouth to her chest.

There is a split second when he imagines that Lena will guide Jordan away from the beach.

And then they begin to dance—horrible and wild. Flailing. Gesticulating. Flinging themselves about as if they are being tossed from a moving train.

He's never seen his mother dance. That was before his time. But now he knows why her career didn't flourish. Another lie he has been told. Another deception.

Because look at them. Look at their spastic bodies. Their lack of rhythm.

Look at his mother corrupting his wife, no concern for the blood on her body, the baby she's lost, the child that has been stolen from them.

From him.

Fury rises in him, anger like he's never experienced before. Uncontainable, it emerges from his throat with a battle cry.

LENA

A roar from the grasses.

"Someone is watching," Luz says, suddenly at Lena's side, her lips against Lena's ear. "I told you someone is always watching us. Someone or something. We have to be vigilant."

Lena lets go of Jordan's hand, watches her spin away, more beautiful with each revolution. She trains her gaze on the grasses.

She can sense it too.

She can smell it.

Something in their midst. Something rotten and insidious.

And then it emerges—a bird of prey. Red-eyed. Talons bared. A violent beat of its wings.

It swoops down from the dunes, across the sand, toward the fire. Its claws wide, straight for Jordan.

DREW

He grabs her. The startled look in his wife's eyes, like she has never seen him before. She swats him off, thrashes and flails in his grip.

She smells of blood and rot.

She bites his arm.

Drew twists her away from the fire. She kicks his shins.

She snarls and spits. His anger grows the more she resists.

He knows he is hurting her. But he has no choice. No choice but to wrestle her away from this madness.

LENA

The bird has Jordan in its grip. The sharp edges of its talons raking her skin, dragging her. Tossing her this way and that. Turning her into a rag doll.

Its predatory eyes unblinking.

Lena pounces, tearing at the creature. She wrenches its claws apart.

It snaps at her—beak clacking.

She reaches for its face, her finger in its beak. She feels its jaws crack. She flings it to the ground.

It shrieks—wild, ferocious, and deadly.

The women stop their dance. They circle her and begin to clap.

How easily they had pulled her apart two nights before, revealing the Lena hidden inside her brittle shell.

She has the same strength. She yanks the bird's feathers, grappling for a wing.

The bird shrieks again.

Lena is not afraid.

DREW

His mother, more savage than anything he's ever seen before. She pounces, ripping him free from Jordan, her hands clawing at his mouth. Her fingers tearing at his hair.

"Mom."

Drew falls to the sand. He scuttles away and tries to stand.

"Mom."

But she lunges again—she's on top of him. Her eyes wild, an animal cry in place of words.

LENA

The rake of talons.

Blood and spit.

Her hands digging into the bird's feathers, yanking and yanking until she finds the weak spot in one of its joints. She grabs a wing and twists. A crack. The wing hangs loose.

The bird's miserable howl—so much like Drew's childhood cries. His neediness that she had submitted to only to have him cage her.

She twists the wing once more.

Another cry.

The bird flails, the impotent flap of its massive, broken wing.

In the bird's place, her son—a terrified, furious look on his face. Furious and fearful.

How many times had she soothed him as a child only for him to grow into an adult who would diminish her?

Lena dives forward, reaching for the bird's other wing, ready to snap it in two.

DREW

Pain that is worse because it comes from his mother.

His arms, both useless.

Powerless to stop her.

Powerless to do anything at all.

The women gathered around her, chanting and singing.

The women, the last thing he will see.

Always the goddamn women.

LENA

The bird is immobilized. And that could be the end of it. But the time is past for half measures. It tried to steal Jordan. And there is only one punishment for that.

Lena straddles the creature, pummeling. Hearing the crack and shatter of bone. Thrilling to the blood spatter from her own fists.

She can feel the fight going out of the beast. It grows limp beneath her. Its shrieks reduced to cries. Reduced to whimpers.

Black feathers sprayed across the sand.

The women cheer and clap. But the sound seems far away, as if it is coming from a different world.

Lena's brow is drenched in sweat.

She wipes her eyes.

There beneath her is Drew, his face battered. His arms broken. There he is—the bird of prey who tried to drag Jordan away. The beast who caged her. The monster she brought into this world.

She reaches down, a hand on either side of his neck, and twists and twists and twists.

When she is done, she rises, her work complete.

And the women rush in to finish what is already finished.

Hair and bone flying free. A bit of scalp—Lena catches it and places it on her head and dances and dances until the sun rises and she falls to the sand.

HEDY

Outside the cave everything is reduced to shadow. The air smells of blood and salt. I cannot tell whether it is day or night.

My sight is almost gone. Just a glimmer at the corners of my eyes, a flicker of something I can't quite make out.

What I feel is silence. Absence.

A scattering.

There is no bonfire. No song. No dancing. If there are still women here, they are sleeping or hiding.

I trip and fall to my knees. Carefully, I crawl across the sand, fumbling as I will fumble for the rest of my life. The last light, about to go out.

What are we good for if not speeding up our own demise?

I feel sand and charred wood. I crawl over a sleeping body. I feel her hair, her face. She is no one I know.

By the sound of the waves, I understand I am heading toward the water.

I cross another body. This one groans. Someone else I do not know.

I hear a seagull. I smell the water, more pungent now that I'm drawing close.

The next body I find does not move. My hands trace arms and legs sprawled and splayed in unnatural directions. I nick my finger on protrusion of bone through skin.

I run my hands upward and find a man's face and know whom I have found.

No breath left in him.

A new sound—the sound of packing. Tents coming down. The clatter of utensils.

My ears have become my eyes and I see the scene in my head— the women breaking camp, abandoning Drew's corpse.

I hear them shuffle away. I hear them groan under the weight of the things they carry.

I hear the sun come up.

It takes me an hour to find the cave again. Inside I can see once more. The man remains shackled.

I watch him leak his golden blood. If I unchain him, he will give me sight.

But it will be temporary. Because here's something I've learned— pleasure is always fleeting and darkness waits in the wings. We are all losing our sight in different ways. Lena, Jordan, Drew—all of them already blind to their lives although they believe their eyes are open. So what does it matter if I can see? I see better in the dark.

I knew it was a lie from the get-go, what Luz told me. But belief is my favorite drug. So I let her trick me. Sometimes you have to push yourself too far to know where you belong. Like Lena—pushing herself to the point of destruction with Stavros, sticking it out to prove that she'd chosen the wrong world.

Still, I hesitate. My hands on his manacles. Because all that vibrancy and color. All of it, mine for the taking.

But no. The sight he gives is only a trick. An exaggerated illusion of a world that doesn't exist.

I choose darkness.

JORDAN

You could say I knew all along that there was no monster. But that would depend on your definition. What's riches to some is poverty to others. It's all a question of perspective. Just ask Drew, if that were possible.

Feral gypsies.

Powerful sisters.

It all depends through which end of the bottle you are looking.

Anyone halfway decent at venture capital or private equity knows that to invest or overtake you can't look at a property from one angle alone. The forward-facing appearance might be very different from what goes on in the boardroom.

And yet, despite your research or your promise of best practices, there is usually some collateral damage from a takeover or a buyout.

The damage is strewn all over the beach. The carnage of last night—not just Drew's broken body, but Lena's exhausted figure too. And Luz and her pack drunk on their bloodlust.

What they don't understand—Lena and I will go on.

We will return to the hotel.

We will clean up. We will gird ourselves in our designer clothes and blow-dry our hair. We will get our nails polished. We will paint our faces with neutral colors and emotions. We will return to America grieving but intact. All this horror nothing but a nightmare carried out during a party that got out of hand. A collective hysteria that we could not prevent. We will relegate ourselves to the periphery. Bystanders. Powerless.

I sit at the edge of the water in my bloodstained clothes.

The monster is gone.

Are you surprised I didn't want it?

Did you ever ask me, Lena?

Or did you assume that because I am rich, because I am tough, because I am educated, my choices were my own?

Or did it thrill you to think that I'd make the same mistakes as you?

Maybe you are surprised a woman like me made a mistake. That I didn't have a voice to say no.

Does that scare you?

Maybe it should terrify you that things break unevenly against women—still after all this time.

Maybe you were hoping that it didn't have to be that way for everyone.

Or maybe you wanted to watch me be brought down.

I wade in the sea up to my waist, rinsing and rinsing and letting the salt water sting and sanitize.

I see Luz walking toward me. For a moment, I imagine pretending

I'm still under her spell. I imagine luring her into the water. I imagine drowning her.

But like I said, Lena and I will walk away. Luz will have to run. And keep running.

I watch her survey the scene, then head to her tent. I imagine she is packing up.

rise from the sea. I am cleansed.

Lena is still sitting next to Drew.

Is she amazed by what she has done? She should be.

I want to tell her to sell the penthouse and the Victorian. I want to tell her to be free. But I know better than to tell her what to do.

I take her hand.

LUZ

What do you see in the aftermath?
When the sun rises?
When the lights come up?
When you realize this was just a warehouse?
A muddy field?
A strip of sand?
When the music stops?
The strobes cease?

Do you see the person you were before—in the mad heart of the dance? Or are you the one stepping away from that skin? Already assimilating to the muted tones of the everyday?

How long will you pretend?

How long can you?

The party will move. The scene will change. New music. New drugs. But at the core, the desire will remain the same.

I reveal yourself to you.

I show you what you refuse to see.
What you do with that knowledge—isn't up to me.

There was blood on the beach.
   But that's not my fault. That's yours.
I'm just the conductor.
The tour guide.
I hold up the signs for you to follow.
But I don't drag you or pull you along.
I am the portal, not the path.

Pick your god.
   Pick your demon.
Pick your house of worship.
Pick your salvation and your downfall.

You'll always come back to me.
   I'm there in the music. In the memory. In the anticipation.
   I'm there when the hairs rise on your arms and the beat flutters
in your chest.

I'm Mama Ghost after all. I'll take you where you need to go.
   And then I am gone.

ACKNOWLEDGMENTS

This book is here today because of my incredible editor, Daphne Durham, who told me to take it to the edge and then farther. As always, thanks to my wonderful agent, Kim Witherspoon, without whom I'd be lost in many ways. Thanks to Jessica Mileo and Maria Whelan at Inkwell. And to Aranya Jain at Putnam. Thanks to Chantal Corcoran for the gift of hospitality and time. I'm so grateful to my early readers: Louisa Hall, Robin Wasserman, and Emily Beyda. And, of course, to my best readers, Philip and Elizabeth Pochoda. I had a lot of questions about everything from business to rave culture to hotels—which Daniel Ezra, Simon Reynolds, and most importantly, Matt Stewart were kind enough to answer. No small debt is owed to Darran Tiernan, who encouraged me to run with this wild idea when I was at sea and to whom I will be forever grateful. Family comes from the most surprising places, and I'm beyond thankful for the one I found with my colleagues at University of California Riverside's low-residency MFA program. I love you all. This book would not exist without my teachers Paul O'Rourke and Victor Marchiaro, who taught me classics and taught me to love classics. Their memories live on in these pages.

Photograph of the author © Darran Tiernan

Ivy Pochoda is the author of five critically acclaimed novels, including *Sing Her Down*, which won the LA Times Book Prize. She won the 2018 Strand Critics Award for Best Novel and the Prix Page/America in France, and has been a finalist for the Edgar Award, among other awards. For many years, Ivy has led a creative writing workshop in Skid Row, Los Angeles, where she helped found *Skid Row Zine*. She is currently a professor of creative writing at the University of California Riverside–Palm Desert low-residency MFA program. She lives in Los Angeles.

VISIT IVY POCHODA ONLINE

ivypochoda.com

LadyMissIvy

IvyPochodaAuthor